THE ARTIMUS BOX

Mike Downs

To Ginni

Best Regards

ISBN 978-1468140415

Copyright 2011 Mike Downs

all rights reserved

Author's Note

Please keep in mind that this is a work of fiction. The names, characters, organizations, and events in this novel are a product of the author's imagination, or are used fictitiously. Any resemblance to actual events or persons living or dead is purely coincidental.

The name Miles Gupton is used with the permission of Penny Gupton, and is my tribute to a friend.

Acknowledgements

The first person in a long list of people who are helping me to achieve my dream of a writing career is my wife Kathy. She is tireless in her efforts to help me along. The cover art is but one of her many talents.

The short list:

Phyllis Gurney, for her unbounded enthusiasm and encouragement.

Kas and Peggy Kastner, for their editing and copy reading, but mostly for their friendship.

John and Patti Shaver, good friends, always willing to help.

Bob Smith, for the course map to turn one.

My gratitude to the readers, thank you. You are the main players.

To everyone with the passion to run at the limit, keep the dark side down.

I toast you all.

Chapter 1
1932 Los Angeles California

Tim knew he was running for his life.

The deep shadows on the street jumped out as the moon danced in and out of the cloud cover on this cool L.A. night. Tim Wahl was the last man to leave the shop. Outside the door, he fumbled with his keys, darkness made it difficult to find the right key to lock up. He was later than usual, but Tim was used to long hours working for Harry Artimus. He was on his way to take the wooden box he made for Harry's latest masterpiece to the boss's apartment.

He wanted to show Harry he had the skills needed to make him a permanent part of Artimus Engine Works. The boss would see his careful crafting of the box. This would surely earn him a place in the machine shop. Harry had only the best men working for him and Tim longed to work alongside them. The slim blond-haired boy was just getting started in the racecar business and he was yearning to show Harry that he deserved a place with the men he idolized.

He walked down the deserted block, his mind fixed on visions of the future. Tim snapped out of his daydreaming when by the glare of a streetlight, he saw three men up the street watching him. He immediately recognized them as the same men he saw arguing with Harry in the shop's office. The men were coming toward him. One of the men shouted to Tim in broken English, "Halt boy! We must speak, Halt!" Tim turned to run. He heard a gun shot and felt brick dust sting his face. The men would have a clear shot if he tried to get back to the shop.

It was a cool night but sweat was breaking out over his body. His heart was pounding hard in his chest…his legs began to tremble. The gunfire terrified Tim. It did not seem real to him, that someone would shoot at him here. He was home in the city he grew up in, not some battlefield. Tim never fired a gun, the Great War had ended before he was born. He knew now the men were after the box and would do anything to get it. Tim did not need to be able to speak their language to know they were killers. He had been a fool to take the box out of the shop, now he was going to have to run for his life.

Tim passed by a new building going up on Washington Boulevard on his way to work every day. He thought if he could just make it there, he could lose them in the huge piles of building materials and the heavy machines. He could find a place to hide in all the construction work. After they quit searching for him, he could go to the police. He would still have the box to show Harry. He would be safe…everything would be all right.

He ran down the street, his pounding footsteps echoing in the quiet night. He slowed and turned down the dark mouth of an alley. Tim began taking quiet steps to the building site. He looked for a safe place to hide in the darkness of the lot. The huge piles of

THE ARTIMUS BOX

building materials and the machines were gone. The lot was cold, still, and very empty. The construction crew must have cleared the entire lot during the day. The steel beams of the upper floors were in place and there were wood planks forming temporary floors. At ground level, wooden forms enclosed the support beams, ready for the construction crew to pour concrete that would provide the foundation.

The shock of realizing the lot was empty froze Tim to the spot. His legs turned rubbery. Rough guttural voices carried in the stillness…the men hunting him were closing in. For the first time in his life, Tim felt real panic. The hair on his neck bristled with sweat. His shoulders tightened, he could almost feel a long rifle sighting in on him. His eyes darted over the empty lot.

He searched for some kind of cover, but he could not see anywhere to hide. The fear coursing through his body was consuming any rational thought. He wanted to be free from this crippling fear, to be safe, but he could not see any place to go. He had to run---he had to climb. The boy clutched his treasured box tightly under one arm and pulled himself up to the first floor steel beams. He crept cautiously on a steel I-beam to a corner to try to find cover behind one of the big vertical beams.

Shots rang out with brilliant flashes of light. Darkness closed over Tim, he dropped with a dull thump to the dirt below. A cloud of dust billowed up, and then settled silently over the body.

Tim's hunters faded into the darkness when dogs began to bark, lights snapped on, and people peeked out from the neighboring buildings. Men dressed only in pants and tee shirts, women in robes, their hair up in curlers poured from the houses. All eager to see something extraordinary, maybe gangsters at play, blood in the street.

Chapter 2

Present Day Los Angeles

It was a cold beginning to a gray overcast day in Los Angeles. The morning fog hung in the air like a dank sheet.

Workmen, holding steaming cups of coffee, gather together in animated conversation at a secluded corner of the lot. An idle backhoe sits in another corner of the foundation. The men are talking about a skeletal arm protruding at an odd angle in the rubble of concrete that the backhoe had ripped up. Blue uniformed police are securing the area. Bright yellow crime scene tape snaps in the cool breeze. A few reporters are milling around impatiently waiting for some kind of story.

The building was another of those great old brick two story buildings built in the early thirties to house businesses on the ground floor and tenants above. No matter how much people wanted to save the artistry of the past, the future must prevail, so the beautiful old building was coming down. New blood was moving in again and new buildings had to follow.

A young patrolman calls his report into the department. The Captain in this small division station receives all reports and decides what action to take. Captain James Stoneham, is a veteran of thirty-five years of police service. Over the years, he has grown heavyset and balding. His gruff exterior sometimes hides the protective nature he feels for his men, and his division. The door to his office is seldom closed.

Van Taylor is the Captain's best detective. He relies on Van's experience the man does not coast. After all the years in service, Detective Taylor still works hard at the job. Stoneham is concerned that the detective is thinking too much lately about retiring, he is not ready to let Taylor go. The Captain knows the man needs a rest but this should be an easy case, a quick one to put away.

Captain Stoneham sits behind his old scarred wooden desk passed down from previous generations. He has kept it as a reminder of the men who sat behind it before him. The cigar burns that mark the edges are from the hard-boiled chiefs of a bygone age. He checks the current caseload and looks at the duty roster. The roster tells him the time Van checked out. He leans back in his chair and studies the view from his window. "Ah, hell, this one's easy." He picks up his phone and dials Taylor's number.

The phone rings incessantly. Van Taylor has gotten just about four hours of sleep. He had been chasing bad guys into the early morning hours and thinks the phone is still a part of the dream he is having. He untangles his legs from the covers and reluctantly answers the phone.

Van is not new to the game; he has been an L.A. detective for twenty-eight years. He is a healthy six-foot tall man with thinning iron gray hair, and at 200 pounds, he thinks of himself as being overweight.

THE ARTIMUS BOX

Van's stand out feature has always been his deep blue eyes. From childhood, people have commented on the intensity of his eyes. Van has found to his delight over the years, that women look into his eyes with fascination also. Now close to retirement, he has earned some privileges.

While still a member of the L.A.P.D., Van is working in a small division headed by Captain Stoneham, his long time friend and mentor. He did not like the fact that the Captain had decided that he would get this gig. It was too early in the morning on a freaky cold L.A. day.

What he knew from the brief phone conversation with his boss was that a demolition crew found a skeleton with a bullet hole drilled through the skull. The remains were in some new construction on Washington Boulevard.

By the time Van got to the scene, the forensic people had already taken the remains out of the old concrete flooring. Under the body, they discovered a wooden box.

It was rough in spots, but still with some polished surfaces. The box, about fourteen inches square, was unopened in a large clear plastic evidence bag.

The first thing Van needed to do was to identify the body and determine when the murder had occurred. The body had fallen, or been placed into a foundation pit and was then buried in poured concrete. Most remarkable was the condition of the remains and personal items. The police found an old pocket watch and a wallet with a still legible 1930 California driver's license issued to a Timothy Wahl with the remains.

Van calls in to check with the department to see if they had any record of a Tim Wahl. The woman in records could not find anything on Wahl in her computer. Records that old would be in file boxes downtown. She thought that Van might have better luck with the newspaper morgue. They still kept old files on microfiche.

Van had not eaten breakfast and knew a place near the paper that still served real buckwheat hot cakes and eggs, with the eggs basted just the way he liked them. L.A. may be a crime capital but it still offered some old time comforts twenty-four hours a day that you could not find anywhere else on the West Coast. With all of the changes Van had witnessed during his lifetime in L.A. (and not many to his liking) he still loved this city. After satisfying his appetite Van is off to the Times building to check the morgue for clues as to the identity of Mr. Timothy Wahl.

He identifies himself to the newspaper morgue custodian, and takes a seat in front of a computer screen. The custodian instructs Van in the use of the program operation. The department keeps the detectives updated in the operation of computers, and new programs in order for them to be able to access the information so vital to police work. Van kept up on his computer knowledge, he has found to his own surprise that he likes computers and new electronic gadgetry. He finds the newspaper program easy to use.

Van decides to start with the year 1930, the date of issue on Wahl's license. After scrolling through the years of 1930 and 1931, he comes to an article in 1932 to do with the disappearance of Timothy Wahl. Wahl's mother, and his employer Harry Artimus, had reported him missing.

Apparently, from what the article reported, his employer was very disturbed by Wahl's failure to be at work. Artimus had sent his entire work force to look for him. The years went by without any sign of Timothy Wahl. Searching the paper in the years after the disappearance, he could find no mention of Wahl. Van finds reams of stories about Harry Artimus. The name Harry Artimus brings back memories of his visit with his wife Kathy to Palm Springs. He thinks it must be the same Harry Artimus, who built all those fabulous racecars.

Kathy Taylor is a very pretty woman; she is a five foot six inch dynamo with short black hair that has some streaks of gray she does not hide. They have been married for twenty-five years. She is, by Van's own admission, his guiding light. She persuaded Van to take some long over due vacation time to attend the vintage races in Palm Springs.

Kathy's grandfather was a racecar driver in the 1920s and 30s. He had given his pictures and sizeable trophy collection to Kathy before his death. Van had always been a fan of auto racing and particularly of early West Coast racing.

It had been a fabulous spring weekend in Palm Springs, the air clear and the weather warm. Van and Kathy stayed at a beautiful old hotel. They relaxed by the pool, and hiked a few of the mountain trails. They took the tram almost to the top of San Jacinto Peak. The floor of the tram rotates to give fabulous views. The tram, packed with sightseers from all over the globe, swayed back and fourth over the sheer cliffs of Chino

Canyon. Kathy squeezed Van's hand for the entire 15-minute trip to the 8500-foot high mountain platform.

When they arrived at the racetrack, Van commented that the variety and number of cars attending was amazing. The people displaying the cars were extremely gracious with their time. Many of the cars at this event were vintage sports cars. Some dating back to the pre World War One era. The cars were on display for everyone to see. The different designs from era to era were readily recognizable to the most casual observer. The very early cars were tall, high off the ground with huge engines. A few had chains and sprockets down the flanks to drive the rear wheels. The later cars became low and sleek, wind cheaters built for speed.

The scene unfolding in the warm pleasant sunshine was of a big picnic party. Brightly colored tents dotted the landscape. There were huge trucks that carried six to eight cars. The trucks had awnings that extended out from the sides with the cars displayed under them.

For many of the people here, the spring event had become the big annual family outing. They came from all over the country to play. Palm Springs was warm and the winter had been a long cold one. Fathers and sons tinkered with the cars. Mothers and daughters set out food and snacks on small tables. The opposite roles took place in some families, with the women driving the cars. On display for all the cars were plaques to describe the car's history: the races won or famous drivers who piloted them. Some families dressed in the period costumes matching the era of their cars.

A row of food venders along one side of the lot had various foods, ice creams, and drinks on display. The desert lot was one big party. The beautiful people came to posture and pose. Irish wolfhounds, groomed to perfection, led their stylish masters on leashes.

Old white-haired men climbed aboard their trusty race cars to roar out on the makeshift racecourse and relive the glory years. A trained ear could tell which era of car was on the course by the sounds it made. The sights, sounds, and smells could put the senses in overdrive.

Kathy walked with Van through the rows of cars. She smiled knowingly when Van darted away to see some new source of fascination.

The owners of the cars had lavished many hours of loving care and considerable money on the sparkling beauties. Most were willing to share the histories of their cars and their own experiences. The cars that really turned Van's head were the cars that Harry Artimus built. These were by far the cream of the crop. As one proud owner told him, Harry's cars were made by the best craftsmen in L.A., if not the world. The man boasted that in the 1920s and early 30s some 6500 man-hours went into the building of each one of these cars. Between 700 and 1000 hours were dedicated to the fantastic finish work that Harry demanded his cars have.

The man bubbled over with Artimus chronicles. He told Van that Harry Artimus was a fabulous and well-loved character. He suggested that Van might want to read more about old Harry. He said there was a great deal of historical data on Artimus and his cars, as well as some of the wild inventions that Harry had thought up that were years ahead of their time.

At the end of the weekend, some of the cars owners invited Van and Kathy to enjoy glasses of champagne with them. They listened to the excited voices of different groups that gathered around and recounted vivid stories of their racing adventures. They stand together and watch the sun sink behind the mountains that surround the desert.

As Van reminisces about the wonderful weekend, he flashes on the old wooden box found under Wahl's remains. He is anxious to get back to the department to see if forensics was finished with the box, so that he can get a look inside it.

Chapter 3

Van drives back to the department to check in. Captain Stoneham and Van have been working together since Van joined the police department. Stoneham had been on the force for years by the time Van joined. He taught Van the street cop lessons you did not get at the academy. Over the years, they have cemented a strong bond. Van wants to tell him what he has found out about the remains, and get down stairs to the evidence room. He taps on the doorframe to the Captain's office and enters to give him a brief run down.

The Captain listens to the excitement in Van's voice; he reminds him of the pending cases they have.

"I gave you this one to go easy on you. Don't make a big deal out of it, boyo. The thing is over seventy years old for Pete's sake. We've got bigger fish to fry."

"Captain has the word; I'm not looking to make it a career. I'm kinda' looking forward to finding out how Harry Artimus figures into this."

Van leaves the Captain's office and heads for the stairs of the old, but well-cared-for building. The well-worn stairs creak in protest as he pounds down the steps.

At the cage opening of the evidence room Van signs out the wooden box. The forensics techs have already opened the box, checked it out for content, and duly signed it over to evidence. He takes the stairs up the two flights to his desk in the squad room and sits down with the box on his desk.

It is heavy, but makes no noise nor rattles from inside it. The beautifully made box feels solid. Someone had spent a lot of time making the box and polishing the cherry wood to a luster that still shines in places. Van notes that the tech dusted the box for any prints and that the tech had taken time to wipe off the dust. Only a small amount of residue remained at the seams. It was unusual that a tech would take the time to do that.

The box has a brass clasp on the side with a small push button to open the top. He pushes hard on the button and is surprised the top opens without much force. On the inside of the box lid is a brass plaque with the inscription, ARTIMUS DESIGN.

Inside are six large wheels set into a barrel-like aluminum cylinder with a strange keyboard beneath the cylinder. There are numbers and letters on the keyboard but neither a complete alphabet nor a complete number set. The keys still work although very stiffly. As they are depressed, the wheels rotate. He notes that the box has some kind of sockets on the inside of the bottom. The metals in the box and the ivory on the key pads are exquisite. The artistry of the work is a marvelous treat to study. The polish and finish have obviously taken many hours of hand filing and fitting to achieve this level of perfection. Van is surprised when he notices other officers gathered behind him.

THE ARTIMUS BOX

"What'yer got there man? The newspapers already got a big story and pictures of the forensic geek show'in it off. Reporter says it's a treasure box, cause why else would somebody take it to their grave. Looks like some kinda toy, don't look like a treasure box to me."

Van turns in his chair to see the men looking over his shoulder. "You yahoos don't know real craftsmanship when it's staring you in the face. Any of you guys even know who Harry Artimus was?"

One of the group spouts, "Musta been some perp you nailed for jay walking back in the day. Maybe the dude was like Rube Goldberg, make'n gizmos. Looks like some kinda gizmo, huh guys."

Van shakes his head. "Surrounded by clowns and the vastly uninformed as usual. You guys got anything to do? I can find you some work."

He turns his attention back to the box, and wonders what purpose it served. As he works it around in his head, he decides to call his better half to see what thoughts she might have.

Kathy Taylor has a large embroidery business in Santa Monica. At times, the details of running the place are almost overwhelming. Jenny, her secretary, goes to Kathy's office to tell her Van is on the phone for her.

For Kathy this is a welcome relief from the hectic calls she normally deals with. Van is not a frequent caller. He gives Kathy a description of his morning, and tells her why he had to run after the early morning phone call from the Captain. Kathy, who also has a passion for auto racing, raced a 1955 MGTF herself in vintage racing. Over the years, she has become acquainted with many people in the vintage racing circles.

She tells Van that she knows a man who is very knowledgeable about early racing. She says he is a real aficionado of Harry Artimus. His name is Phil Manley. He owns a premier vintage racecar restoration shop in Long Beach. Kathy says she will call Manley and set up an appointment for Van to see him.

Van would like to email Phil a picture of the box to see if he could give some idea of what he was dealing with.

Signing evidence out of the department on a new case requires a lot of paperwork. This is not one of Van's favorite things to do. In Van's language, the paperwork is a major ass-burn.

Kathy calls Manley to ask if he would have time to check out Van's email. Phil replies that he is eager to see the pictures. He tells Kathy that he has never heard of Harry having a company named Artimus Design. Kathy calls Van back, she says to send Phil the picture, and gives him Manley's email address.

Van takes a digital picture and sends the email to Manley. He tells Manley he needs to know what purpose the box served. He also asks for any details Manley might have on similar work Artimus undertook.

In the meantime, he decides to check the police morgue to see what progress they made on the remains of Tim Wahl. Reilly Flynn is the coroner's assistant, he is a rail thin man who speaks with a small soft voice. Van has worked with him on cases in the past; he calls him to get a progress report.

The short story is they are behind, as usual. Reilly tells him that he will give him a heads up within two days. Van decides he has done enough for the day so he takes the box and signs out to go home. He was thinking of taking the box home to show Kathy. He walks out of the squad room with the box. Van stops on the stairs and thinks about the paperwork he should do, he decides instead to leave it in the evidence room.

It is a short drive from the cop shop to Pacific Palisades, but not without plenty of traffic.

At home, he opens a bottle of cabernet and goes out on the small deck he and Kathy built in the back yard to enjoy the wine and wait for Kathy to get home. He wants to turn in early to make up for the early morning. He calls the pizza place to have them send a deep dish special.

The next morning he is up and feeling refreshed from a good nights' sleep. Kathy is still sleeping so he makes some coffee as quietly as possible. While the coffee is brewing, he does his usual exercises, then showers, shaves, drinks his coffee and is out the door to get off to work.

As he nears his car in the driveway, he stops short. There is broken glass on the ground next to the 1962 Morris Traveler he has just finished restoring. The door window is broken. Van looks to see if there are any fingerprint smudges around the window or door and looks in the car to see what is stolen or damaged.

This is a good neighborhood in the Pacific Palisades. Van inherited the house from his mother and father's estate after they died in an automobile crash some years before. Van was their only child; his father was a metallurgist with the same Los Angeles steel company for forty years.

Van's father expected him to follow in an engineering trade, but he could not get his head into the mathematics. After his military service, police agencies recruited him, along with many of his fellow grunts.

He liked the work. He felt he could do his part to make a small patch of the world a better place. He still thrives on bringing the bad guys to justice through his work as an investigator.

There does not seem to be anything missing from the car and no damage other than the door window. Van cannot understand why someone would just break the window and not take the radio or the CD player he had put in. Both of the audio devices were high-ticket items.

Van cleans up the broken glass. He drives down the hill to his normal breakfast stop. The small diner has been in the business of feeding hungry locals for forty-odd years. When he walks in the door, the aroma of fresh coffee and bacon cooking make his stomach growl. The place is another of Van's favorites. Today it will be a spinach scramble to make up for the grease of yesterday's breakfast. Back in the squad room, Van sits at his desk wondering who would have gotten a kick out of vandalizing his car.

He boots his desktop computer to check the morning run up of current cases and emails. One of the emails is from Phil Manley. In the email, Manley tells him that he needs to see the box at his shop as soon as possible. The box could be the key to a long-time rumor regarding Harry Artimus and the German government that goes back to the early 1930s. He did not elaborate any further. Van is not much interested in the rumors but does want to know what function the box had. He needs to know what it might have to do with Wahl's murder.

THE ARTIMUS BOX

Out come the forms in triplicate Van has to fill out in order to get the box out of the evidence room and away from the department (more ass-burn). He pokes at the keyboard with his two forefingers. Way too much fun.

Van signs out an unmarked Crown Victoria car from the motor pool for the trip to Manley's place in Long Beach. Traffic is not as bad as it can be, so Van makes good time. He is thinking on the way that he still has to order a window for the Morris.

He finds the shop on Cherry Ave. and, after parking, he goes inside to find Manley. The building is an old wood structure. It has a high arched roof with an exposed beam ceiling. The building has a feeling of the great work done there. The divided workspaces are neat, clean and well lighted.

There is only one car in the shop---it looks to Van as if Manley's business has seen better days. The car is one of the Harry Artimus' front-wheel drive cars. It seems to be almost completed. As Van studies the car, he finds himself fascinated by the mechanical genius that Artimus incorporated into its design.

Most fascinating to Van are the front-drive transverse gearbox, inboard brakes, and drive shafts. The artistry Harry Artimus incorporated into the design work and the finish were unprecedented. The old wood building, along with the smells of oil and machinery, are a pleasant tribute to the men and machines of years past.

Phil Manley introduces himself to Van; he has the look of a man who is troubled. His pallor is pale, his face is haggard, shadowed with a three-day beard. With his stooped posture, he looks as if he is bearing a heavy weight. Manly cannot take his watery eyes from the wooden box Van is holding. Van is looking forward to a tour of the shop with tales of the cars and drivers. Without any preamble, Phil ushers him into his office and shuts the door behind them. Phil stands behind his desk, he asks Van to place the box on the desk so he can open it. Van sets the box on the desk, he watches Phil open the box. The expression on Phil's face is one of wonder and expectation. As soon as Phil sees the inside of the box, he breaths hard and looks up at Van.

"This is the real thing" Phil exclaims. "I never thought I'd see this, I thought it was just a wild rumor."

As Phil seems transfixed Van asks, "Do you know what the box was used for or why Wahl would be buried with it?"

Phil says that he thinks the box was an encoding device, a forerunner of the enigma machine the Germans used in World War II.

Van has read the British accounts of the enigma machine. It was a very complex device used by the Nazis to send encoded messages to the various Nazi commands. The messages were almost indecipherable to anyone not having a decoding machine. The keyboard keys activated discs that rotated to change the letters on the message. The decoding machine on the receiving end changed the letters back to decipher the message.

"I know Harry was of German descent but I never believed he would be involved in doing anything that would work against America. Harry was extremely patriotic. I have no idea how it would be related to your murder, but if you'll leave it with me I can scrutinize it more thoroughly and be able you give you a better report."

"Sorry," Van says. "I can't leave it with you. It's evidence in my investigation; you can take some pictures of it while I'm here if that will help you."

Manley is reluctant to give the box back to Van. He places the box on a table to take some digital pictures. With the box open, Phil works his hand into the interior. Van does not want the machinery disturbed. He is about to voice his concern when Phil looks over his shoulder at Van, and quickly removes his hand. He continues to take pictures from different angles.

Van asks if he can get a tour of the shop but Phil says it is a bad time, he is far too busy now. Van picks up the box, but as he turns to leave, Manley calls out to him.

"Why don't you come back sometime in the future? I'll give you a tour of the shop, and you can keep me updated on what's going on."

Van thanks Phil for his help and walks away. Van is just at the door when Phil calls out again, "I don't think the box is worth much to anyone but an Artimus collector as it is, but take good care of it. Let me know when you're finished with it, I'd like to buy it so I can add it to my collection. I don't want to fight with the other collectors. I'd appreciate it if you could give me the first shot at it."

"Sure thing Phil, and thanks for the help."

Oh yeah, not worth much, Van thinks, yeah I'll bet. He climbs into the Crown Vic to make his way back to the station. As he starts to back out of the lot, he gets a call from Captain Stoneham.

"Van, we just got a report that your house was broken into. One of your neighbors saw some strangers walking around your yard. The neighbor could hear noises from inside the house. They saw Kathy drive off earlier and knew you had left. When they called the Palisades P.D. the cops were on it in minutes.

"When they got to your house the neighbor told the cops the perps left on foot before they got there. The neighbor didn't want to follow them."

"Captain, when I went out to my car this morning someone had broken out the door window of my car. Now the house gets broken into, that hasn't ever happened before. I think someone is looking for something. I've got a funny feeling maybe this box is worth big money. You should have seen the way Manley pawed through it. I get the impression from Manley that other people are interested in the box. You know the Wahl murder is the only new case I've got that has any high-buck evidence. I've got the box with me, but I just signed it out this morning."

"Van I don't know about the break-ins but I can't see that it has anything to do with the Wahl deal."

"Yeah, you're probably right. I can't see it either, Cap. I just don't like coincidences."

"Well, buddy boy, I know you want to take a look at the home front, but get back as soon as you can. We have a ton of current cases that need work and, as you insist on working without a partner, you need to get on back here and take up the slack."

"Cap, I'm still in Long Beach. By the time I get home and see the Palisades cops, the day will be shot."

THE ARTIMUS BOX

"Okay boyo make it an early start tomorrow and check with me in the morning. Let's put our heads together and prioritize the case load."

"Can do boss."

"And, Van, I hope your house is okay."

"Thanks boss."

Van leaves the Morris in the motor pool garage until he can get a replacement window so he drives the Crown Vic home. Traffic is a killer; there is no short cut on surface streets. Marina Del Rey is now a parking lot, so is Lincoln Avenue. The San Diego freeway is stop and go, or more like stop and stop. It is almost four o'clock by the time Van pulls in the driveway.

The Palisades cops have dusted for prints, and left a card with a number for him to call when he gets home. Van checks the front door lock; he sees no sign of any damage. He walks around to the back of the house and finds the rear door locked also. As Van continues around the back of the house, he finds the small bathroom window screen and the window lying on the ground. The perps destroyed the screen, but the window is intact, just out of its channel.

The black powder residue shows that the police dusted the window and frame. Given the state's last round of budget cuts, these are the last of the real service police. Van knows he is lucky to live here.

He unlocks the front door to go into the house. It is not as bad as it could be. Some books and chairs are upset. All of the drawers and cabinets have been gone through everywhere in the house, but the plasma TV and the DVR are still in place. Nothing seems to be missing. Van wonders what in the hell is going on here. The only damage other than the screen is that whoever broke into the bathroom broke the toilet tank lid and cracked the tank as they came through the small window opening.

Man, Van thinks, somebody is definitely after something and it all seems to have started with this box. I may be nuts but I'm going to take this to the bank and lock it up.

The bank is three blocks down the street so Van puts the box in a paper sack and walks out of the house. His neighbor comes out of her house next door.

"Is everything okay Van?"

"Not much damage Alice thanks to you. I appreciate you calling the cops. I think it would have been a lot worse if they spent more time in the house."

"I saw a man outside your house on the sidewalk. I think he was watching for the police. I'd never seen him around here before. I thought I heard noises in your house so I called the police."

"Thanks again Alice you did the right thing. Take care, I've got to go."

Once in the bank Van goes to the manager to ask if he can store the box until tomorrow morning. The bank manager says no problem; the Taylor family are customers of long standing. The manager gives Van his safety deposit box key, and they walk together to the safety deposit room.

Van returns home to call Kathy so he can relay the news of the break-in. After hanging up the phone, he wanders around the house putting things back in place.

THE ARTIMUS BOX

Chapter 4

After getting things in order, Van turns on his laptop to start looking for information on Harry Artimus. Hearing Manley say the box was probably not worth much makes Van certain that something is not right. Maybe he just wants it for his collection, or maybe it really is worth big money. It could be worth more than Manley can afford at an auction.

The information on Artimus is staggering. There are books, newspaper articles, patents, and photographs from the turn of the twentieth century to after World War II. However, Van cannot find anything that leads him to any information about the box.

Most of the people that were involved with Artimus are gone, as in deceased. The people that have researched Artimus, who are still alive and actively writing are small in number. One such person, a Mr. Donner, seems to be a wealth of information. He lives somewhere in Santa Monica.

Van will look him up tomorrow, right now he feels like a big steak dinner. He fires up the BBQ on the deck. Van expects Kathy to be home from work soon.

Van takes a big Harris Ranch steak from the refrigerator to marinate. Next, he slices up some potatoes, sweet potatoes, onion, and carrots. He puts them in a large baking pan. He sprinkles them with salt and pepper, fresh rosemary, adds plenty of good olive oil and puts them in the oven to roast. He marinates the steaks with gold tequila. Van opens a bottle of Merlot and goes out to the deck to cook the steaks on the grill.

When Kathy comes home from work; she finds Van on the deck with a wine glass in one hand and a long handled metal spatula in the other. She puts her arms around Van. On her tiptoes she whispers in his ear, "I love you…and even more when you cook."

A loving wife, a great meal with a good wine, Van knew he was a lucky man.

Van pours Kathy a glass of wine and she brings out plates and utensils.

"Honey," Van asks, "do you have any ideas about Harry Artimus or how he was involved with the box?"

Kathy sips her wine and says, "I haven't heard anything about code machines or anything like that associated with Artimus. His cars and engines are world renown for their clever designs. I know he had a bunch of patents for mechanical devices. I think they were things like carburetors, and transmissions. I suppose that the kind of mechanical coding device you described would have been within his grasp.

"You did say the box had a plaque with Harry's name on it so it must have been made by him or at least in his shop. He made almost everything in-house; only major castings and some heat-treating were trusted to vendors.

I do remember reading that Harry once said that he had a mystical control of some sort. He said some of his ideas came through this control.

THE ARTIMUS BOX

"One book I read stated that he was able to finish the sentences of other people he was talking to before they could finish them. I take it that some people found it very strange when Harry started talking about his control and his ideas. There are plenty of tall tales told about old Harry, some make him sound kind of zany. He's a legend. I don't know how many books have been devoted to him. What did Phil Manley say about it?"

Van takes the sizzling steaks off the grill. "He says he thinks it's an encoding machine, and not worth much. That doesn't seem right to me. I need more information. I found a Malcolm Donner on the internet who seems to be an Artimus authority."

Kathy replies, "I've met him and I can tell you he does know a great deal about Artimus. He has at least one of the cars Artimus built. He got one of the Jack Novac cars out of Europe after World War II when no one else knew of it or, for that matter, seemed to care. I would bet if anyone knows about the box it would be Donner."

Van says, "I'll find the address and phone number for Donner tomorrow and set up an appointment. The boss wants me on some other cases so I might have to put this on the back burner for now. I'll make you a deal. I'll clean things up if you go and make yourself sexy to show your appreciation for such a fine dinner."

Kathy says, "You've got a deal stud but don't complain in the morning if you can't walk."

Van is up early and swings his legs out of bed to test their steadiness. He decides he can walk and is off to the shower. Van has some coffee, bolts out the door, and drives off to work after a quick stop for fresh bagels.

Traveling down West Sunset, he has just gotten to the switchbacks by Will Rogers Park when a big SUV pulls in front of him. Another SUV hits him from the back pinning him in. Van immediately radios dispatch.

He is identifying himself to the dispatcher as a police officer when three men with ski masks come at the car. As he turns his head to watch the men go to right side of the car, a fourth man breaks the driver side window with the butt of a shotgun. Shattered glass rains in, peppering Van's face and hands.

The man with the shotgun sticks the barrel of the gun through the opening of broken glass. He orders Van out of the car. Van slowly opens the door leaving the radio keyed in hopes the dispatcher will send cops in a hurry.

One of the men opens the right side door and starts looking in the car. He looks under the seats then goes to the back seat. Another man grabs the keys to open the trunk. Now all the men, except the man holding the shotgun on Van, are pulling the car apart looking for something. The man with the shotgun barks at the other men to hurry up.

One of the men says, "There's no box here, man."

The man with the shotgun says to Van, "Okay, dipstick, where's the box?"

"Box, what kind of box are you looking for?"

The barrel of the shotgun moves to Van's face. "The Artimus box man, don't screw with me."

"The Artimus box? We've got a wooden box in the evidence room at police headquarters," Van answers. "Do you guys know I'm a cop?"

THE ARTIMUS BOX

One of the men says, "Nobody cares you're a cop. Where's the box? It ain't in the evidence room."

Van says, "I don't have it man. If it's not in the evidence room I can't tell you where it is."

The same man says, "You're a liar, asshole. We know you got it. Maybe we got to go back to your house to get it from that fine little woman."

The man with the shotgun, obviously the head of this group, yells "Shut up you idiot. Don't say nothing till I say so." He looks at Van and says, "Give it up or the wife is the next on my list."

Van says, "You go near my wife and it will be the last thing you will ever do."

Shotgun man says, "You think I give a damn? You ain't nothin' to me pig."

Blaring sirens are getting close. Van turns his head to see how close the cops are. The butt of the shotgun slams down hard on the side of his head. He goes down on his knees, his head exploding with pain, light flashes, then it all goes black.

Chapter 5

Van regains a foggy consciousness. He cannot seem to focus, he blacks out again. He hears voices but cannot make out what they are saying.

He slowly opens his eyes, but as soon as there is light, there is pain. Van tries to open just one eye. He opens the eye just enough to let in some light. The light is blurry and far too bright. He thinks that maybe it would be better just to rest a little.

Voices are filtering through the pain and starting to make some sense. Someone is talking to someone else; they seem close by. One person is telling another person that the blow was hard enough that there could be complications, lack of something, pneumonia, and something else.

Van's head is clearing; he gets one eye open but cannot seem to open the other eye. The harder he tries to get the eye open, the more it causes his head to pound with pain.

A man in a long white coat leans over him, "I'm Doctor Gordon, you are in a hospital. You have sustained an injury on the left side of your head. Your left eye is swollen shut. Can you tell me your name?" Van mumbles.

THE ARTIMUS BOX

The doctor examines Vans opened eye to see how it tracks his hand, satisfied he says, "While this is a serious injury, we have done a scan that looks good. The scan doesn't show any permanent damage. You could have a hard time talking or eating for a little while."

Van now sees the Captain and Kathy on the other side of the bed. He starts to talk, but has trouble moving his mouth. He tries to talk with his jaw closed. It comes out as a kind of mumble. "Got ta keep kath zafe."

On the second try, it came out, "We've got to keep Kathy safe. Oh, man, can you get me something to write on?"

Kathy, tears streaming down her cheeks, is holding Van's hand in both of hers.

The Captain gives Van his notebook and a pen.

"Take it easy Van. Just give me what you can, so I can get a grip on what happened to you. Do you know who did this to you?" Van tries to shake his head no, and feels his brain rattle in his skull. There are more bursts of light and pain.

Van writes on the paper no, they wanted the Artimus box. That's what the guy called the box. The head guy had a shotgun. He said he's coming after Kathy.

The guy thinks she has the box or can make me get it for him. We have to keep her safe now. I'll write up a complete description of the four guys and the vehicles, but please make sure Kathy is safe. You know how stubborn she is.

The Captain says, "You don't have to worry. I'll have men posted everywhere she goes and one of the police women will stay with her at night until you are fit to take care of her yourself."

"The attack on you makes it certain the Artimus box, as you call it, is what the break-ins have been about," the Captain points out, "but I still don't get why a box from 1932 is worth this much trouble.

"Write out as much as you can. I'll put on everyone I can spare. I don't like my men beaten down, or threats made on their families. And just for you, me boyo, I'll have your friend Al Lieber posted with Kathy. Nobody is gonna mess with the biggest, baddest cop on the payroll. That means nobody will mess with her while big Al's looking after her."

The Captain leaves Kathy in the room with Van and goes to phone orders into the department. Kathy is still holding on to Van and looking at his face. Van mumbles, "It only hurts when I breathe." Kathy laughs and says, "Well you do look good in a turban."

Van starts writing a description of his assailants but only gets a page done before he falls asleep. Kathy takes the pen and paper and puts them on a table next to the bed. She hates seeing Van hurt and wonders who did this to him and why.

Chapter 6

The Captain returns to the room, and quietly ushers Kathy out to meet with Al Lieber. Al is a huge man at six feet four inches and 275 pounds; he generally fills any room he comes into. He is light complexioned and has a choirboy's face of young innocence. Van befriended Al when he was new on the job. He helped him through the first learning years with his own on the job experiences. Al and his petite wife, Ann, and almost anyone would look petite next to Al, have been to Kathy and Van's house on many occasions to help them remodel or to watch a game or a Formula One race on the plasma big screen.

"Is Van Okay?" asks Al.

"He will be with enough rest," Kathy replies. "The Doctor said that Van was struck with enough force to have caused brain damage but the tests did not show any internal swelling, or bleeding, and that's a good sign. He needs some time to recuperate and be monitored by the Doctor to make sure there are no complications."

"Man I want to find the guys that did it," Al exclaims.

"Al what you need to do is make sure no one tries anything with Kathy," the Captain says gruffly.

"Nothing is going to happen to Kathy on my watch Cap," Al replies.

"I want to talk to Malcolm Donner," Kathy says. "He may well have the answer to what the attraction is to the box."

"Who is Donner?" asks the Captain. "What does he have to do with the box?"

"He's written four or five books on Harry Artimus and sourced a lot of the people Artimus worked with," Kathy replies. "He may be the only man alive that has an answer to why the box is so important."

"Kathy do you want to stay with Van awhile, or go home?" asks the Captain.

"The Doctor wants him to rest, so I'll go on home for now and check back with the hospital staff in the morning. I'll come back as soon as they will let me in to see him," Kathy replies.

"I'll get a run down on your Mr. Donner," says the Captain. "When I locate him I'll send a detective to interview him and find out what he knows."

"Please, let me talk to him," pleads Kathy. "I've already met him and I can really be more help in questioning him. We can discuss Harry Artimus together as fans of his work. I can get him into the subject of the box when he is into the moment. I think that will be far more productive, and because I'm familiar with the names and places, I can get to the subject of the box and I'll know if he doesn't know of it, or if he does and is holding something back from me."

"I don't think it's a good idea to expose yourself when we know the bad guys are looking for you," the Captain replies.

THE ARTIMUS BOX

"I'll take Al with me. I'll call you when I see Donner and when I leave him," pleads Kathy. "I know I can get more information from him than a detective. I've been active in racing and I know the subject. You know I'm right about this Captain. I want those guys that hurt Van."

"Al, take Kathy home in a police cruiser and don't let her out of your sight," orders the Captain." I'll have a policewoman meet you there. I have officers in place to watch Van's room 24 hours on four-hour shifts. We can decide on a plan of action in the morning, Kathy, call me in the morning okay?"

The next morning Van struggles to open both of his eyes. When he can focus, he sees Kathy and Al Lieber in the room with him.

"How do you feel?" asks Kathy

Van replies "Well, the throbbing in my head is much less, to answer your question. I'll tell you I'm glad to be able to see out of both eyes. Man I need the license number of the truck that ran over me. Good to see you Al. Thanks for coming to see me."

"I'm Kathy's guard," Al says. "You know you can trust me not to let the bad guys near her. I'd just like to get my hands on them."

Van tells them that he has finished his description of the men that attacked him in a long and detailed report for the Captain.

In the report, Van noted that the men all wore heavy boots and had long chains securing their wallets. He takes this to mean these guys might be part of a motorcycle club or gang. In addition, he questions how the men knew he had the box, and that it was not in the evidence room as he told them.

The attackers seemed to know a lot about him. They knew his car and his house, and he was pretty sure they were the same people that broke into both his house and car.

"You look so much better honey," Kathy notes as she holds Van's hand and looks at him with concern. "I hate the thought of you being so hurt, but we'll get those guys."

"We, what do you mean we?" asks Van. "I don't want you anywhere near those guys. They would hurt you just for sport. Those four guys are lowlifes, they're the stupid muscle in whatever is going down. I don't think by any means they're the brains. Someone sent them after the box. We need to find that person and if we find why the box is valuable, we'll be a lot closer to who wants it."

"I just called the Captain," Kathy says. "He's set up a meeting for me with Donner."

"Oh come on Kathy, will you please stay out of this," Van pleads. "I'm telling you, baby, the guys that attacked me will hurt or kill you without a care. They'd enjoy it."

"Van," Kathy puts her hands on her hips and retorts, "I'll have Al with me. I'm the best person to talk to Donner and you know it."

"I know how hard headed you are," blurts Van. "I don't want anything bad to happen to you. Please promise me you'll be really careful and not be foolish. You can't set yourself up to take the heat. Al can't be everywhere and four against one is still bad odds. There were four guys that attacked me remember."

"Four against one!" Kathy snorts. "You're not counting too well. I can take care of myself."

THE ARTIMUS BOX

Before Van can answer, Al chimes in, "I promise I won't let anything happen to her Van. I'm going to take extra precautions and I'll get a couple of the guys to be with us at Donner's place."

Van groans, "Al you know how stubborn she can be, don't let her out of your sight. I'm counting on you man."

Chapter 7

Malcolm Donner lives in a beautiful old courtyard bungalow two blocks from the beach. The type of bungalows that was at one time popular with the early film stars. In Santa Monica real estate today, the property is worth a fortune. Al has detailed two more men around the place so that no one can go in or out unchallenged. Kathy and Al have planned it this way so as not to spook Donner.

Kathy rings the doorbell and is greeted by Donner and invited in. The entrance to the house is like an old movie set. The walls are in a rich dark wood trim with colorful tapestries. Malcolm Donner is the handsome leading man. He is tall with a mane of perfect white hair. His face sports a neatly trimmed Vandyke. He wears a brown smoking jacket with a red collar. To complete the look, he has a red silk ascot. Kathy thinks back on their first meeting. They were at a vintage race meeting in Northern California wine country and Donner was dressed in a dress shirt and blue jeans. This Mr. Donner at home was quite a different animal.

He leads Kathy into an enormous study that seems too big to be in the same house. The walls have shelves brimming with books and racing memorabilia. A silver

THE ARTIMUS BOX

tea set is on a small table between two very comfortable looking red leather chairs.

The silver tea set is an actual trophy from an early Culver City board racetrack.

Kathy goes to the table and says. "What a lovely tea set."

"Thank you, I got it from an estate sale. It always reminds me of the tracks we used to have around here. You may not be aware of the board tracks."

Before Kathy can answer, Donner launches into a descriptive.

"In 1924 a business group constructed a wood board track in Culver City. The track was a high-banked oval that drew over 100,000 spectators to the first race held there. It thrilled masses of people with racecar speeds of 136 miles per hour.

The races were spectacular events---board track racing could be extremely dangerous you know. The construction of the tracks consisted of 2x4's laid on edge. Each facility required a minimum of a million board feet of lumber. After a few years the boards became brittle, the floors splintered, and then went to pieces. The tracks were too expensive to maintain. The rising value of real estate coupled with the cost of maintenance soon made the tracks obsolete.

All of the board tracks in America soon disappeared, and paved and dirt oval racetracks replaced them. Oh excuse me, I do prattle on a times."

Donner seats Kathy in one of the red leather chairs and pours tea for her.

"It is a pleasure to see you Ms Taylor," Donner croons. "I enjoy conversing about Harry Artimus, but tell me, if you would be so kind, why a police Captain would call to make an appointment for me to speak with you?"

"Well sir," starts Kathy.

"Oh no, no. You must address me as Malcolm, my dear," Donner exclaims.

"Thank you Malcolm," answers Kathy. "It's a long story but the crux of the matter is we have a crime associated with an Artimus connection and my husband is the investigating detective. My husband Van asked me if I knew anyone that would have information about Harry Artimus. I immediately thought of you and told my husband that you are the foremost authority on the subject of Harry Artimus and his work."

"What is the nature of the crime if I may ask?" asks Donner.

"If you could please bear with me Malcolm," replies Kathy. "The nature of the crime is still confidential. If we can just have a pleasant chat about Harry I would be very grateful."

Kathy and Malcolm Donner spend the next hour talking about Harry Artimus. They have tea and pastries. Malcolm shows Kathy some of the trophies and memorabilia he has collected over the past forty-five years.

They chat about the engines and cars Artimus built. Kathy then steers the conversation to the mechanical devices Artimus conceived.

Malcolm is enjoying the center stage and is showing Kathy some drawings from his Artimus collection when he stops in mid-sentence, asking, "Is this about the Artimus box?"

Kathy takes a moment before she answers. "Well, yes, I do need to know what the box is. What can you tell me about it and why you suddenly thought about it?"

"The box is a hot topic lately," Malcolm says. "I have had a number of emails asking for information about the box in the last two days. Some are supposed to be from accredited authors. Others from people I have never heard of. It is not a subject without anger on my part. Ten years ago, this house was broken into and my collection ransacked. The robbers took a book I had of Harry Artimus drawings.

That book contained the only partial drawing of the box that I know of. You may know Harry had drawings made of everything he did. This was the only drawing I have seen that had not been completed."

At that instant, an explosion rocks the house. Noise and smoke come from the front room of the house. A spray of fog flows from a sprinkler system in the ceiling that quickly smothers the flames.

Kathy heads toward the front room when Donner shouts, "Stay here please, don't go into the room yet. The room fills with Halon gas, a fire depressant. There will not be enough oxygen for you to breathe for a minute or two."

There is pounding at the front door. Outside Al Lieber is yelling. Malcolm Donner asks Kathy to be calm. He says, "The rooms in this house are all protected with the best fire and intruder systems made. After the break in ten years ago, I had the systems installed.

The Halon fire system emits a gas that robs fire of the oxygen it needs to burn while leaving no mess behind to destroy my books and collections. It's the same gas used in racecar fire systems. The Fire department and Police are connected to the system; they will be here any minute."

Just then, Kathy hears sirens wailing and getting close. Exhaust fans go on in the front room to clear the room of smoke. Malcolm goes to the front door; he opens it to find Al Lieber readying himself to try to break the door down.

"Are you a policeman?" asks Donner.

"Yes" Al says, "Where is Kathy?"

Donner, looking puzzled, says, "She is fine." He is about to expound on that when Kathy appears.

"What happened?" asks Kathy.

Al answers, "An SUV stopped in front of the house. I was on the way to see why it'd stopped when a window of the SUV slid down and some sort of grenade launcher poked through the window. It fired a grenade through the front window and took off. At almost the same moment, a shutter of some kind inside the house closed behind the shattered window. I ran to the front door to try to get in only to find the door locked. I was frantic to get in. I was about to try to break it down when the door opened. I've got to call the Captain now that I know you're all right."

Police and Fire department personnel are quickly on the scene. Malcolm Donner proudly shows them how his systems work.

After the excitement died down and the Police and Fire department people leave, Kathy and Al, with the other men stationed outside, look at the damage to the front room of the Donner house. They are amazed to find that the front window the grenade smashed through and large area of the floor where it landed and caught fire are the only points of damage they see.

THE ARTIMUS BOX

"Malcolm I am so sorry," Kathy says.

"Is this connected to your visit?" Malcolm asks.

Kathy answers, "I'm almost sure it's not a coincidence, but I have no idea how anyone would know I was here. Al, could someone have followed us?" Kathy asks.

"I don't think so," Al says, "I watched for a tail but I didn't see anyone."

Kathy turns to Malcolm and says, "I feel terrible about this, but I really need to know anything you can tell me about the box. The box is the key to all of this and so far we know practically nothing about it."

Al stations himself by the front door. "I'm going to stay here with you," he says. "Van told me not to let you out of my sight. He'd kill me if I let you get hurt."

Donner does not seem very upset with the fire bombing. "The shutter will stay down until I have the window replaced. I know I should be angry but I am actually quite pleased with my intrusion systems. But let me explain the little I know about the box.

"Sometime in early 1930 Harry was approached by a man and asked to build a four-wheel drive car that he could take to Europe to race. Harry did not know the person and had not heard anything about him through the racing grapevine. The man was full of charm and flashed plenty of money.

"Harry agreed to build the car and he began the design process. The design exercise required a full complement of drawings. It is in this group of drawings that I found the partial box drawing. The information about the car stops in 1932, at the same time the drawings stop.

"In 1964, I interviewed Harry's draftsman, Leo Deerman, a wonderful man with a talent for detail that complimented Harry's design ideas. Harry would many times just talk about his ideas and leave Leo to do the design work as well as the drawings. I was very curious about the four-wheel drive car. I wanted to know what happened to it, so I asked Leo if could tell me about it. And, if he could remember anything that could give me a clue as to where the car might be.

"Leo said he remembered the car because it had caused a big argument in the shop between Harry and the shop foreman, a man who's name was Fred Offlower. Fred respected Harry a great deal and Leo had never heard them argue before this.

"The reason for the argument, Leo went on to tell me, was that Harry wanted the car, which was sixty percent completed, destroyed immediately. Fred said that was crazy, that they could just dismantle the car and use the parts in other cars they were building for other customers, or sell it. Harry was very angry, not with Fred, who was like a son to Harry, but with the person who commissioned the car.

"I asked Leo," Donner continues, "why Harry was so angry. Did he know why? I do not remember the conversation with Leo verbatim but the story was something about the man that commissioned the car knew of Harry's mechanical genius. He wanted Harry to make a machine that could be used for enciphering messages.

"The machine was intended, so the man said, for his business. This would keep his competition from being able to read his communications to his suppliers and retailers.

THE ARTIMUS BOX

"Harry somehow found out that the man was not who he said he was. The story was that the man actually had no use for the car. He just wanted to trick Harry into making this code machine. Harry was a mild-mannered man, so it was unusual for him to be so mad that he would want to see good work destroyed."

Kathy struggles to hide her disappointment, "Can you tell me if the man was ever identified, or if there are any leads we can follow to find out more about him. Is there any more information about the box itself?"

"All I know" replies Donner, "is when I asked the same question of Leo, he said the name given him for the drawings was Kline Bearing Company. He assumed the man's name was Kline. The incomplete box drawing Leo started was the most interesting part of my interview with Leo.

What Leo could remember was that after collaborating with Harry on the initial details of the mechanism, Harry stopped the process and Leo did not have enough information to continue.

Harry continued to work on the project at home. Leo knew Harry had directed a young apprentice to make a fine wooden box for the mechanism. That is all of the information I have been able to find on the box. Until now I have not had an interest to pursue the matter further."

"Why would Harry take the work home?" Kathy asks.

Donner muses briefly before replying, "I think because he did not want anyone to know what he was doing. Harry owned a ranch of over one hundred acres in Malibu Canyon and he had a workshop on the grounds for his personal use. I am intrigued with all of the interest I have received lately. I will resume research on the box and on Kline to see what I can find."

"Please be careful Malcolm," cautions Kathy. "These people are dangerous. We don't have a clue who they are. I need all the information I can get, but not at your expense." She gives Donner a kiss on the cheek.

"You've given me plenty of information to follow up on, thank you very much. Please keep me up to date with any new information you find. Take care Malcolm."

"Do not worry about me, I am owed recompense," Donner proclaims. "I am not afraid of bullies."

Kathy calls Captain Stoneham to give him an update. She asks if there could be any old records about the Kline Bearing Company. Or if not the company, would there be any records on Kline.

The Captain says that he will put the records people on it. This could take some time he explains, as the records people already have a large backlog of searches.

Chapter 8

After going home from the hospital and several days of lying on his back, Van grows restless. Kathy wants him to rest and stay away from work. He thinks of the time lost on his caseload and decides he is ready to get back to it. Van phones the Captain.

"Have you been able to find any information on Kline, Captain?"

"Are you sure you're ready to jump back in? I can spare you for more recoup time."

"No sir I'm ready to get to it. I'm going nuts watching the tube."

"I'm not convinced you're ready, but we've found a record of an assault from late 1932 that names Horst Kline as the assailant. What's really interesting is that the person who filed the complaint was an employee of the Artimus Engine Works. The report states Kline struck a man named Jos Vermane with a cane when he couldn't answer Kline's questions.

"Kline was reported to have three witnesses that placed him miles away in Burbank at the time of the alleged assault and he was not questioned further. The police filed the report because two weeks later Vermane was beaten and left in an alley in Venice on his way home from work. He claimed Kline was responsible but couldn't prove it.

"Harry Artimus went to the police with a story of kidnapping threats and extortion by Kline. Artimus was angry, he wanted Kline arrested. The cops got a warrant to arrest Kline only to find that he had left the country on a ship bound for Germany."

"Does that leave us with any way to follow Kline's trail or find out more on the box?"

As the Captain leans back in his chair and looks at the growing pile of files on his desk he says, "The box is the key. We have the box, it's up to us to find out what makes it worth fire bombs and threats."

"Cap, with your permission, I have a friend who can disassemble the box and tell us what secrets it may have."

"Can he do it nondestructively Van?"

"If he can't, no one can. You've met him a few times but maybe you'd feel better if I told you a little more about him?"

"Okay shoot Van. I need to get going. I have a meeting with the Santa Monica cops on what we have for their Donner bombing investigation."

"I'll make it short Cap. Miles Gupton is an old friend, we were in the army together.

Miles is also a car racer. He owns a business machine shop in El Segundo. He fixes all kinds of machines and he knows racing. The nationwide business machine manufacturers have been trying to get him to work exclusively for them for years. He designs his own machines; the guy is a mechanical genius but won't take orders from anyone."

THE ARTIMUS BOX

"If he can be trusted Van, you can take the box to him. I don't want the box harmed but I want you to take it easy. I'll have Jim and Brad pick you up and go with you. Don't leave the box with your friend, and report to me as soon as you can."

"I trust Miles with my life Cap. He's the best guy I know for this."

Van is back in the saddle; he has two officers assigned to him on temporary duty. He calls Gupton to see when Miles can look at the box.

Miles is a few years older than Van and very much a free spirit. He and Van, in the years before Van married Kathy, traveled the world, partied, boozed and womanized. Van considers Miles his best friend.

Van picks up the phone and dials, "Hey Miles how's it going, man?"

"You know me Van, right as rain. Kathy called to tell me they let you out of the hospital. I was worried they might commit you to the psych ward but I guess you lucked out again."

"You're a mile of smiles as usual pal."

"Yeah, well, I did call every day to see how you were. I knew you'd be okay when I heard the only injury was to your rock hard head."

"Okay Miles, I know you're buried getting your new shop location going. You still working fourteen hours a day?"

"Make that sixteen to eighteen and that, my friend, is the pleasure of owning your own business."

"I've got a favor to ask Miles. I need you to take look at a box that Harry Artimus made back in the early 1930s."

"Is that the same box that got you beaten up Van?"

"Well yes it is, but I know you're an Artimus fan and the internals of this box are fascinating. The box is some kind of encryption machine. I don't know much about it or how it might work. What I need to find out is why the box would be responsible for one murder in 1932, and break-ins and fire bombings today. I know you're the man to dissect it."

"Okay but I'm up to my neck right now. Can we make it after six tonight? I'll buy the beer? You know how to find the new place?"

"I know right where to go. I'll see you at six and I'll bring enough Rolling Rock beer for you and me and the two officers assigned to baby sit me."

"Whoa, you need baby sitters now; maybe you need to ply me with some that special red wine you get from up north. Danger is my business but only when I'm well paid."

"What kind of danger are you seeing in the business machine game? Did you get a paper cut this week? Okay, never mind, I'll put you on the Christmas list."

Van and the two officers, Brad and Jim, go to the bank and pick up the box. From the bank, they head down to El Segundo. As they turn on Lincoln Avenue, Brad, the officer driving the unmarked Crown Vic, says to Van,

"I see a black SUV following us that is the same one I saw across the street from the bank. The SUV made a "U" turn behind us when we left the bank and is four cars behind us now."

"How many people are in the SUV Brad?" Van asks.

THE ARTIMUS BOX

"I think four or five. Can you see them, Jim?" Brad answers.

"Yeah I got'em, four guys.

Van turns in the seat as much as he can and says, "Jim call it in, I want to know who those guys are. Have them pulled over. The local cops can use the firebombing alert as provocation. Brad, I don't want those guys to know where we're going. Take a left on Wilshire. Let's see how soon the cops can pick them up. Jim, you keep the cops posted on our route."

Van's Crown Vic continues east on Wilshire.

Before they have traveled more than a few miles, they see flashing red lights behind them.

Suddenly the Sport Utility Vehicle that has been following Van's team pulls out into oncoming traffic. It is coming by them on the left side of Van's car. As Brad, Jim and Van look on in amazement, the four men in the black sinister looking truck are frantically pulling ski masks over their faces. Oncoming traffic is trying to get out of the path of the huge truck, barreling straight at them. Horns are blaring, cars skid to a stop, as other cars bend metal swerving into each other.

The heavy truck smashes into the side of Van's car forcing it onto the sidewalk. The black vehicle turns right on a side street almost hitting Van's car again and is gone. The cops chasing the fleeing SUV flash by unable to make the turn. Pedestrians and a light pole stop Van's car.

They have a long delay reporting the events to the local police. Van gives them the license number of the SUV.

The local cops take their information and tell Van that the SUV got away. The license number is for a vehicle reported stolen. Van's team continues to Miles Gupton's shop, keeping an eye out for anyone following them.

Villainy, like rust, never rests.

Chapter 9

El Segundo is a small town by the L.A. airport. The town has been a supplier of machinery and parts to the aerospace industry, as well as the auto racing industry, for decades. It is now a sprawling mass of tall buildings and fast-paced businesses.

Miles' new store is in one of the older buildings that was a racecar facility in the 1970s. Miles has completely remodeled the building doing most of the work himself. It is now a show place of fine woodworking with an efficient workspace in back for design work as well as repairs. Miles welcomes Van and the officers into his building.

The style of the foyer is striking. Mahogany and glass cabinets around the room contain early business machines along with many racing trophies Miles has won. Van is eager to start on the examination of the box, but he knows Gupton has worked long hours on his new building and wants to show the place off.

The men tour the facility with Miles pointing out the salient points. Before ending the tour, he brings the men back to the foyer, and opens one of the large glass and wood cabinets. Miles brings out some engine parts that the Artimus shop manufactured in the late 1920s.

The parts are a hand-forged tubular connecting rod, an aluminum piston, and a centrifugal supercharger. The parts are jewel-like in appearance and are a fitting inclusion with the beautiful machines, the racing trophies, and other racing pieces Miles has displayed, in the cabinets.

"Okay Miles, we're impressed. Can we get on with the box?"

"Oh sure, I try to educate you with fine art and a display of talent, but I can see this is lost on you bums," replies Miles.

Van has the box in a paper bag. Brad has the Rolling Rock beer in another paper bag. Gupton brings the men to the machine repair area of his shop.

The repair area is 9000 square feet, with an extensive array of tools, electrical testing equipment, and metal working machines. At the back of the shop is the Lola Mark One small-bore sports racing car Miles is restoring. After rolling a huge toolbox next to a workbench, Gupton takes the box and places it on the bench. He opens the latch to expose the inner workings of the box.

"Wow," he exclaims, "you weren't kidding about the craftsmanship. This is beautiful. It's hard to believe it is over 70 years old. Let's see if we can find how this little beauty works."

Miles tests the keys while he watches the wheels revolve. He then presses each key to observe the movement and function of that key. "I'm going to remove the outside box from the machine so I can see the working parts."

THE ARTIMUS BOX

In a very few minutes he has found all of the retaining screws. After removing them, he lifts the mechanism from the wooden box.

He sets the mechanism on the bench and picks up a small light to inspect the inner gears. After spending some time with the light, Miles switches to a flashlight with a magnifying glass eyepiece. He spends more time with the light before taking a bore scope from a toolbox. Van is fidgeting and walking around the bench Miles is working on.

"Hey Van, will you find a place to sit and be still? You're driving me nuts."

"Okay, but how long are you going to take buddy? You haven't said a word since you started?"

"I'm trying to understand the purpose of this, Van. It doesn't seem to operate as a completed machine. There are electrical sockets on the keys and the shift forks, but no electric source and no way of electrical transmission from them.

There aren't enough keys to display the complete alphabet or numerals. My take on it right now, is that it's actually a prototype to demonstrate how a completed machine could work."

"Are you saying it doesn't work? Why would it be worth so much trouble?"

"Well I can't see why people would kill for it. Any artifact from Artimus is worth a good deal to a collector but not the mayhem you've had. Let me do a sonic test on the shift drum and the shafts. That'll give me some idea of the internal dimensions. Maybe there's more to this, or it could have some internal operation to transmit information. Or maybe, knowing Harry's reputation, it works by magic."

Miles goes to one of the equipment cabinets and brings back to the workbench a small black box with a probe attached by a coiled cord.

"This instrument will tell us the wall thickness of any material," explains Miles, "by sending a sonic wave and retrieving the signal. We can test for solid or tubular, steel or alloy. I'll have to remove the shift forks that the keys move in order to get to the shaft. This is a small diameter shaft so I don't think we will find much here."

Miles applies a lubricant to the shaft, then he places the probe on the lubed spot.

"Nope, this shaft is solid. I'm going to take the linkage apart and remove the shift drum so I can test it." He pulls the toolbox closer to the workbench and begins to remove parts from the mechanism.

Van is nervously pacing. He says to Miles, "Hey man can you put that back together again? I didn't know you were going to completely dismember it."

"Not to worry old chum, this is easy compared to some of the machines we work on. It's a very clever device; part of what makes it so clever is the simplicity of the design."

After removing a great number of small parts, Miles places a splined shaft about 12 inches long and 2 inches in diameter on the workbench and repeats the sonic process.

"This shaft is tubular. The sonic meter registers the wall thickness at .083. This means the shaft has over a 1-3/4" inside diameter. I don't see any end caps so you would assume the shaft is solid. I think I'll drill a small hole in one end and see if there's anything inside the shaft."

THE ARTIMUS BOX

"Hey man, don't ruin that thing! The Captain would kill me if he could see all the parts on your bench and that silly grin on your face. Is this your idea of fun?"

"Don't worry. I'll put it all back together, and if the end caps don't easily come out, I'll stop. Just tell me if you can see anything in this so far that makes this valuable, because I don't."

"Okay, okay, man, get on with it and stop with the evil grin."

Miles drills a small hole in one end of the splined shaft. He then uses his magnifying light to look into the shaft.

"Hey man there's something in the shaft; I'm going to enlarge the hole so I can insert a puller and remove the end cap."

Van, with sweat on his brow, just rolls his eyes, but he does know his friend is the best guy in L. A. for this work.

Miles clamps the shaft in a special soft-jawed vise, and inserts a very small puller into the end cap. He grins at Van and snaps the puller. The end cap pops free.

All of the men lean over his shoulder to peer inside the shaft. Heavy grease fills the inside of the shaft. This type of packing grease keeps the metal parts from any corrosion.

Miles reaches into his toolbox and takes out a long handled spoon. He begins to remove the grease from inside the shaft. He pulls the first spoonful out of the shaft and knocks the spoon on the bench top to deposit the lump of grease. He flattens out the lump of grease to be sure there is nothing in it. There are no parts or pieces in the grease.

Inserting the spoon deeper into the shaft, he removes a larger amount of grease, and repeats the spoon knock on the bench. This lump has large glass beads mixed in with the grease.

He takes the lump and places it into a screened basket; he then places the basket into a degreasing solution.

"Okay man, what is that stuff?" asks Van.

"The grease is a preservative and was used in this case to keep the particles from rattling inside the shaft."

"Come on man, what are the particles? I don't care about the grease."

Miles laughs and shakes his head, he is clearly enjoying the moment.

"Why, my old friend, this is the stuff dreams are made of."

"If you don't stop fooling around buddy, you're going to wish this was a dream."

"Van, my lad, you have no sense of humor. The sparkly things are diamonds, of course. The shaft may be full of them."

Miles removes all of the stones from the shaft and cleans them in the degreasing solution.

"That should put an end to the big mystery for you buddy. I think those stones are blue diamonds; they should be worth a lot of money. I'll put the machine back together for you."

"Man, you sure put me through the wringer but, and it pains me to say it, there's no one better for this kind of job than you, laughing boy."

THE ARTIMUS BOX

"Why, thank you, I did enjoy myself. Watching you sweat made the work good fun. No really, I enjoyed getting a first hand look at the inner workings. Artimus was up to something with this thing. He didn't want the diamonds to be easy to find, and the machine is far from complete. I admire the workmanship. I really wonder what he was up to."

Van rolls one of the stones between his fingers. "Um yeah, I wonder too. I'll let you know what we find out."

Chapter 10

Van Taylor watches as his friend Miles carefully puts the Artimus box back together. The man has a brilliant deft touch.

Miles is taking each piece he has removed and placing it back in the reverse order from when he took it apart. There is no wasted motion. The man knows where each piece fits, and in what order to replace them.

"Do you want me to put the diamonds back in the shaft before I reassemble the rest of this?"

"No, put them in this evidence bag. I've marked the time and date, but we're going to keep this quiet."

Miles' hands move with precision, each piece he picks up goes into place without a miss-step. There are dozens of small keys, screws, gears, and wheels.

Van and the two police officers watch with fascination as Gupton put the pieces back together.

Van watches the faces of each man as he says, "Someone knows what's put into evidence at the department, and I want this known by as few people as possible. We know everyone at this moment who is aware of the diamonds; I'm gonna report this to the Captain, but if word gets out about the diamonds, it has to come from one of us. Okay boys let's get this back to the department. It's too late to take the box back to the bank, although I think that might be the safest place for it."

"Van you can lock it up here in my safe."

"No can do man. I appreciate the offer, and your help with this. The Captain gave me an order not to leave the box here, and I don't want to put you in danger. There are some bad guys looking for this box and, thanks to you, now we know why.

One of the many questions I want the answer to, is how do the bad guys know what's in the box. The expert we questioned didn't know about the diamonds. I need to see if he can clear this up for me without telling him about what we've found. Right now I'm going to call the Captain to report, and ask him what we should do with the box."

Van goes into Miles' office to call the Captain, "Cap, we've found the answer to the box riddle. In one of shafts inside the mechanism, Miles found nine diamonds. They look pretty big; I'd guess maybe 2 or 3 carats each."

"Damn good work." The Captain says, "That clears up why the bad guys are so desperate to get their hands on the box. The questions I have now are, how do they know what's in the box, and who is the rat in my department? We need answers. Where are you now?"

"I'm still with Miles Gupton in El Segundo, Cap. I can head back to the department when he buttons the box up, in about a half hour."

"Okay. Thank your friend for me and please make sure he understands to keep this under his hat. We need to keep a lid on this. I want to keep track of who knows about the diamonds and the fewer people the better."

"I agree Cap. What do you want me to do with the box?"

"I think the best plan is to bring it back to the precinct tonight. I'll put the key to the evidence room in your top desk drawer. Take an old evidence file box and put the box and diamonds in it. Tell Jim and Brad to report to me tomorrow, and email the evidence box's file name to me. Take the weekend off and rest up. You and Kathy go do something fun. Monday we'll make a fresh start at this case. I'm going to have Jim and Brad go with you to deposit that box in the bank Monday. I don't want to keep it here, but I do want it accessible."

The men return to the police department with the box and diamonds. Van thanks Jim and Brad for the help and he relays the Captain's message for them to report to him in the morning.

Brad says, "Jim and I both had a good time. That Gupton guy is plenty clever, he's a real joker. I really enjoyed the shop tour and the old racing stuff is great. I'd like to know more about that era. It's a pleasure, every once in a while, to get away from police work. Hey, Van, how about a snort at the sports bar before we go home?"

"Thanks, but I've got a dinner date with Kathy."

"Then how about a short one? I'd like to hear more about the old cars and races."

"Hey come on Brad," Jim pipes in, "you've brown-nosed Van enough. Let's go."

Van lets himself into the small evidence room with the Captain's key. The caged room contains shelves with hundreds of marked cardboard evidence boxes. He

THE ARTIMUS BOX

takes the wooden box and the diamonds and puts them into an evidence box that belongs to an old robbery case. First thing Monday morning he will transfer the box under guard to a secure bank vault near the department.

After emailing the file name to the Captain, Van goes to the department garage to pick up his Morris Traveler. The department mechanics installed the new window glass while Van was recuperating. Van enjoys the late night drive home through the hills with the nimble little car. He is glad to be free of the box and to be going home in time to enjoy a late dinner with Kathy.

When Van gets home, Kathy is waiting with a kiss and a glass of Cabernet. They bring this special red wine that is only available in Sonoma back from their trips to there.

"You've had a number of phone calls this evening. Malcolm Donner has come up with some interesting research in regards to Tim Wahl and he'd like to see you as soon as you can."

"I'd like to see him too. Why don't we call him tomorrow, and see if we can meet at his house? Saturday may not be a good day for him, but I would like to see some of his collections."

"Al Lieber called a couple of times to see what you found out about the Artimus box. We are all very curious and I think Al is concerned with your safety too. He wants you to call him as soon as you can."

"Let's have some dinner and I'll tell you all about it, but what I tell you will be between you and me. The Captain thinks the fewer people that know about the box the better; we know someone inside the department is leaking information."

"I'll call Al tomorrow and tell him what I can. If we can set something up with Donner, we can meet with him. We could plan to drive up the coast this weekend to that place in Ventura we like, and have dinner by the sea. You know, Kathy, we could stay at that old hotel in Ventura for a romantic weekend getaway. We haven't just relaxed by the sea for a long time, and it would be nice to walk on the beach in the morning without all the crowds."

"That's what I love about you. You know how to treat a girl right. Work has been so busy and worrying about you has made me cranky, Ventura would be a great tonic.

"After dinner, we can go online and see what more we can find on Harry Artimus. I found some more web sites that have a lot of information on Harry and how he started out with the racing business. I can set it up on the big screen and we can both enjoy the show."

They go to the small room that Van remodeled into a combination exercise and TV room with help from Al Lieber. They have worked together to bring the old house into the 21st century. They completely replaced the old wiring and plumbing over a period of five years. On the rare days Van has some time off, he enjoys the work. Al has helped with the heavy work when the jobs required two men. Van and Kathy have also helped Al and his wife on work they have done to their house. Both men work well with their hands and with each other.

Kathy has done the entire computer set up and added a sound system. She works with computers a

THE ARTIMUS BOX

great deal in her shop and has a full complement of the latest electronic gadgets. They sit down in high backed chairs to view the web sites Kathy has found. The best one they find has a good short summation of Harry's life.

The web site features some old pictures of Harry building carburetors in the workshops that kept getting larger. In the early 1900's Harry's shops were frequently outgrown. In later years, they see some interior pictures of the shop Harry had when he was building everything in-house.

There are more pictures of the racecars and some of the famous drivers that all lined up at Harry's door to get the best cars and engines of the time. After the picture show, there is a short narrative of Harry's life.

Harry Artimus was an innovator as a boy in the Midwest. In the 1890's he was making improvements in farm machinery. As a young man at the turn of the century he moved west, first to San Francisco where he worked in bicycle repair, then to Los Angeles where he worked in a machine shop.

Harry found he enjoyed making various metal parts using the shop's modern machine tools. While machining kept him busy, Harry discovered an interest in the automobile. He was fascinated by the mechanical solutions then in use and he knew he could improve on what he saw.

In early 1914, Harry bought a lathe and a drill press from money he had saved. He rented a small garage and set up his machines to make the automotive carburetors he invented. These carburetors were superior to any currently in use. As Harry's business boomed, he moved to a larger shop in order to be able to produce the orders that kept pouring in for his invention.

A large corporation in New York bought his company and moved the manufacture of the carburetors to the east. With his new wealth, Harry bought the latest machinery, mills, lathes, drill presses, forging equipment and casting ovens. He moved to a new larger building and began experimenting with new metals and casting techniques.

By the mid 1920's Harry had a machine shop known as one of the best on the West Coast. He and his talented crew could make anything to do with engines and cars. Harry perfected the use of his own aluminum alloy to make automotive engine pistons. Manufacturing racing pistons grew into making complete racing engines, which in turn led into the manufacture of complete racing cars.

Harry Artimus, in the early American auto racing industry, was the man to go to for the best-engineered and finished racing engines. In the late 1920's supercharging racing engines had become the way to win races. Harry invented new ways of making his centrifugal superchargers more efficient, and was able to deliver more horsepower than the other racing engine producers of the era. His engines and cars won the Indianapolis 500 year after year.

Van gets out of his chair and stretches. After a big yawn he says, "That was good; I loved the pictures of the interiors of the shops. I get the impression that Harry must have gone through a lot of money.

I'd like to see more, but I'm worn out. Let's call it a night and we can come back to this again. I'll race you to bed.

THE ARTIMUS BOX

We can dream the dreams of a simpler time."

Chapter 11

In 1998, workers are tearing down an old workshop in Malibu Canyon to make room for landscape improvements on the property. This is the site of the old Harry Artimus ranch. The workers are doing the hot dusty work by hand at the request of the owner, Kimberly Derby. Some articles of value from the Artimus family have surfaced on the property and the owner wants to make sure they do not overlook anything.

In one of the walls of a rundown workshop, the workers find a tin box hidden in a recess. The foreman of the job gives the box to the property owner who is supervising the work.

Derby takes the box into his workroom of the extensively remodeled old house. The box has a small locked clasp that is easily pried open with a screwdriver. The man is atremble with anticipation. The box contains pages of rolled up paper. There is clearly legible hand-written script on the paper that has yellowed with age.

The papers are in the form of a testimony of events concerning a person named Horst Kline and written by Harry Artimus.

THE ARTIMUS BOX

The journal begins:

The history of my association with Horst Kline.
By Harry Artimus September 20, 1932

I find a need to chronicle my involvement with a man known to me as Horst Kline. Mr. Kline has contracted me to undertake the design of an encrypting device under dubious circumstances. Should the need arise I will send copies of this journal to my attorney, and to the police.

Horst Kline introduced himself to me in the garage area during the running of the 1931 Indianapolis 500. Mr. Kline informed me that he owns a large ball bearing factory in Germany and has distributors worldwide.

He became a frequent visitor to the garage area. He listened intently to my every word and paid me compliments at every chance. He took me to lavish dinners where there was no expense spared. At one such dinner Kline proposed that I design and build a four-wheel drive racing car with a supercharged 300 cubic inch V 16-cylinder engine for him. He would use the car, Kline said, in the European Hill Climb Championship. He told me that my engines and racecar designs have made me the talk of the European racing fraternity. He said that we are both from the old country, which I took to mean we have German heritage in common.

To make the deal, he told me money is no concern. Whatever the cost, he was willing to pay for the best. Kline said he also had other projects in mind that he would like to work on together with me.

Kline's overbearing manner was not to my liking. I was not impressed with him.

Nor was I from the conversations I had with him on the subject of auto racing or racing engines. He was not knowledgeable and talked nonsense.

However, I do love new challenges, this would mean new engine and car designs. I was also aware that the depression is on in America and this deal would mean security for me and my employees.

I accepted Kline's proposal to build the engine and car with the proviso that he deposit $35,000.00 to my bank. Kline eagerly agreed and wanted to meet with me in L.A. after the Indianapolis race was over. The race was another victory for our Artimus cars. I returned to L.A. by train and went directly to the shop.

I gathered the men together to tell them of the race in Indianapolis and then to bring them up to date on the orders I received after the victory. I asked Fred, my shop foreman, to follow me to the drafting room, where we met with Leo, my lead draftsman. Standing by a drafting table, I outlined the thoughts I had about building the Kline four-wheel drive car and the 16-cylinder supercharged engine.

I must say the beginning of a new project is my favorite part of the job. This is when new ideas are born. This is when I am most alive, I feel like I can conquer the world. I have the best minds and the most skillful hands in racing in the team that works with me. I am up at all hours with new ideas; I rarely leave the shop, and spend the nights there. I only go home for baths and fresh clothes.

Mr. Kline phoned me to make an appointment to come to the plant and discuss the new car. The next day

THE ARTIMUS BOX

Kline arrived in a large limousine and I met him at the main entrance. We shook hands; Kline patted me on the back like an old friend. I asked Kline if he would like a tour of the factory.

I had recently installed a new Italian engine dynamometer that I am very proud of, and was eager to show it to Kline. I ushered Kline into a new room I had built for the dyno.

As I pointed out the features of the dyno, I noticed that Kline seemed distracted; he looked around the room as if he wanted to find something familiar to him. He saw a centrifugal supercharger on a workbench, went to the bench and picked up the supercharger. I did not take Kline's disinterest in the dynamometer kindly, and I found it curious to see that Kline inspected the supercharger with great interest. I was sure Kline was not well versed in the technical aspects of the piece.

Kline asked me if this supercharger is the latest type. I told him that this supercharger was one that I was currently testing with a new type of impeller. Kline wanted assurance that his engine will have the best supercharger on it. He said his car is to have the one with all the secrets.

I told Kline the secret to the efficiency of the supercharger is in the impeller design, and that my team and I are constantly improving the impellers.

Kline said he was anxious to discuss the new car and engine designs with me. I showed him to my office, which is open to the shop floor, but when we were in the office, Kline fidgeted nervously. He wanted me to accompany him to a private club on La Brea Avenue, where he could discuss matters with complete confidence. I did not want to leave the plant, there was so much work left to do, but Kline was adamant.

I agreed to go to his club for a short lunch after which Kline would have me driven back to the plant. We arrived at his club and the manager greeted us at the door. Inside the club, the manager escorted us to a private room. He left us with the lunch menus. The room was large and decorated with Coat of Arms shields on the walls and Knights in Armor stationed in the corners of the room.

We ordered lunch and I told Kline that I needed to be back at the plant soon and asked him to get down to business. Kline chuckled, as he removed a small pouch from his coat pocket. To my surprise, he opened the pouch and poured out a dozen large sparkling diamonds on the table before me.

The diamonds, he told me, are two to four carat blue diamonds from a South African mine in which he has some interest. He said they are valued at more than one hundred thousand dollars. I became more wary of this man but I was interested in what was going to happen next. Kline moved his chair next to mine. He said he knew of my genius in mechanical devices. He said he needed an encrypting device he could use to send messages to his business interests that will be safe from his competitors. I told him that a machine such as this was not anything that I had any experience in designing.

Kline would not take no for an answer. He said a proper device could be worth millions, and that with my German heritage and genius he was sure I was the man for the job. He explained that the development of the device needed to be in secret. He was sure that no one would suspect me of being involved with an encryption machine. Undertaking the manufacture of the encryption device along with the racecar was a perfect cover.

I asked him why building such a machine should be secret at all. He answered that his competitors would be anxious to have such a device for themselves, and if they knew who was working on it they might try to steal it for their own. Kline took a bank receipt from his inside coat pocket and handed it to me. He said he deposited the $35,000.00 for the car to my account that morning. He added that the diamonds would pay for the development of the enciphering machine plus a bonus.

This was too much to ignore. I could not afford to miss the opportunity to take this on. I must say I was very interested in trying something so completely new. The spur of the moment decision was to do it, but on the condition that there would be no time limit within reason imposed on the development of the enciphering device.

We had a pleasant lunch with very little talk about the four-wheel drive car or the engine. It seemed the enciphering machine had much more importance.

I felt very uneasy; money had never swayed me in the past. I felt I should walk away from this man and his machine. The challenge was too great. I told myself I owed it to my company, and my employees to take the job on.

Some events with Kline, since agreeing to do the job, have given me second thoughts. I hope I did not let my ego get the best of me.

Chapter 12

Kim Derby, the owner of the Artimus ranch is elated with the Artimus papers. He hears heavy footsteps in the house and gets up from his desk chair to investigate.

The foreman he hired for the demolition work has entered the house and is looking into each room as he walks down a hallway in his big boots. He is a large man with a torn T-shirt displaying a multitude of tattoos. He wears a red bandana around his head and a chain from a belt loop to his wallet. The foreman has a mop of long greasy black hair and small cruel eyes set into a heavy, bearded face. He comes into Derby's workshop as Derby is putting the papers in a file cabinet.

"Hey man what was in the box? Maybe we oughta make a deal on any stuff we find."

Kim Derby is growing uncomfortable with the questioning. He tells him that the box contained some of the artifacts from Harry Artimus.

"Who's this Artimus guy? Are the papers worth anything?" the foreman asks. The owner shrugs and says the papers are of historical value only, and that the original owner of the property was a famous personality

THE ARTIMUS BOX

in the 1920's and 1930's. Derby tells the man that he wants the men doing the demolition to be careful. He does not want a potential artifact damaged. Derby says to bring anything interesting to him at once.

The man grins bearing ugly teeth. "Yeah I'll take care of anything we find personally. You don't wanta cut us outta nothin', do you buddy?"

Derby is thinking it was a mistake to hire these guys. His friend Phil Manley recommended them to him. At the time, he thought Manley would not have steered him wrong. He is now feeling threatened by the foreman's manner, he waits for the foreman to leave and phones Manley to ask about the men he recommended.

Manley answers Derby's phone call and asks why he sounds so upset. Derby tells Manley of the unease he has about the foreman's threatening manner. Manley asks what he has found that would be of value.

Derby replies that a box of papers was found, written by Artimus and they have to do with a person named Horst Kline.

Manley asks what is in the papers. Derby says to Manley that he is concerned about the foreman; he does not want to talk about what he has found.

"Look Phil we talked about all this before. I don't want to sell any of my Artimus artifacts. You know that. You said you had reliable guys that would help with the demolition. I'm trusting you to keep these guys under control.

I don't mind telling you the foreman you sent just flat scares me."

Manley knows Derby has an extensive collection of Artimus memorabilia that he is not eager to share.

Phil also knows any papers that concern Kline could answer questions that have been lost in time.

"Don't worry Kim; I'll talk to the man. I got him for you because he's a big tough guy that is just the man for your job. His guys have worked for me, they're maybe a little scroungy but they're good workers. So don't worry about the foreman I'll talk to him, you'll be okay."

Derby is not reassured, he knows he needs to be careful about any items found on his property. He is sure he should fire the men that are working the property now, and hire a bonded company.

He returns to his workshop to find the foreman going through his file cabinet. He yells to the man to get out of his house, to take his men with him, and not come back.

The foreman turns to the owner and says, "Don't yell at me. You ain't nothing to me but a little sissy rich kid. Give me the papers we found in that box or I'll mess you up so bad you won't walk for weeks."

The owner turns to run down the hall to get to the phone. He hears the heavy boots coming behind him as he picks up the phone to dial 911. A hand grabs Derby's hair and jerks his head back; a large heavy knife slashes across his throat.

The foreman jumps back from the man as blood spurts out of the severed neck. He laughs and goes back to the workroom for the papers. Next, he goes through the house and the grounds with the help of the other men; they take anything of value. After plundering the estate, the men carry five-gallon gas cans into the house.

THE ARTIMUS BOX

The gang splashes gas on the body of Derby and throughout other rooms of the house. The foreman goes from room to room setting fire to the house; the gang then flees. Great orange flames crackle and soar into the sky as they consume the rich history. All this destruction is to conceal a vicious murder, born of greed.

Chapter 13

Phil Manley receives a phone call at his shop. A newspaper reporter wants to interview Manley about Kim Derby's death. He listens to the reporter's story. Manley, shocked by the news, says he does not know the circumstances regarding the man's death. Although the house burned to the ground, the arson squad was able to determine that someone murdered Derby and deliberately set the house on fire. The arson squad investigation also revealed a ransacking of the house and grounds.

After hearing the gruesome details, Manley realizes this will bring trouble his way. Far from feeling any remorse, he feverishly tries to think of a way out. Before he can keep his mind from spinning, the man who was the foreman on the Derby home walks into the shop. Manley knows the man as Dutch, the leader of a motorcycle gang known as Evil's Revenge.

Evil's Revenge is a group of about twenty members; most of them kicked out of other clubs for being too wild and uncontrollable.

As their eyes meet, Dutch smiles at Manley's obvious unease. Dutch puts his arm around Manley's shoulders and walks him out of the shop to a van in the

THE ARTIMUS BOX

parking lot. Dutch opens the rear doors of the van, which contains a sizeable collection of Artimus objects.

Manley looks in the van. He recoils with a mixture of fear, delight, and fleeting sadness. Manley says to Dutch, "He was a friend of mine. I had no idea you would harm him. I don't want to be involved in this. Take this stuff away."

"Bullshit," Dutch growls, "you're gonna take this shit and pay me $250 grand for it. You sent me to the guy and told me to get any of the Artimus stuff I could. Well man, I got it all.

You're in this shit as deep as I am. If you get nervous and think about going to the cops, I'll kill you and every member of your family, asshole. I read the papers we found in the workshop. That box the papers talk about is worth a fortune. We can both be rich when I tear it apart. Who's got it Manley?"

"I don't know what you are talking about, Dutch."

"Manley, I'll give you the weekend to read the papers and get me my money. By that time, you better know where the box is if you want to stay healthy."

Dutch grabs Manley's shirt and pulls him toward him, "Don't go soft on me pal. Get me the dough. I'll be back Monday morning. Here, take the papers. Remember we're partners in this box deal."

Manley tries to pull his head back from Dutch's fetid breath. Dutch pulls him closer to him and laughs in his face. A much shaken Manley returns to his shop and tells his employees to knock off for the weekend. He goes to his office barely noticing the crumpled papers in his hand.

Manley knows that Dutch and his gang are a serious threat to him and his family. He worries about his business. If anyone finds out that he used Dutch's gang to get Kim Derby's Artimus collection, his business will be in ruin. This is the worst day of his life, his worst nightmare come true.

It is only when he cradles his head in his hands that he notices the papers again. He begins to read the Artimus testimony. Harry's words wash away Manley's troubles. As he reads he becomes engrossed in the text, these are Harry Artimus' own words, in his own handwriting. It is as if Harry Artimus is speaking directly to Manley.

His excitement builds as he reads the text where Harry writes about the enciphering machine.

Chapter 14
The Artimus Journal continues…

I returned from the lunch with Kline full of misgivings. I wanted the job; the challenge of the enciphering machine had already stimulated my brain. I decided to be positive, to take some action.

I telephoned a friend of mine, George Stall, who is a Los Angeles Police officer. We met at the Ascot racetrack some years ago; he had been to the plant on many occasions to bench race with my employees and me. I gave him a brief explanation of the new project and I asked him if he could find any information on Horst Kline.

With that done, I decided to go ahead with the car and engine. After a few weeks, the enciphering machine still troubled me; I was concerned with Kline's motives. That moved me to stop my drafter, Leo, from continuing any drawings of the machine. I took the machine to the workshop in my home in Malibu Canyon to tinker with the mechanism when I had time to spare.

Two weeks after the lunch meeting, Kline came to the plant and asked to see the progress on his project. I took him into the drawing room to show him the drawn plans updated to that time. He took me aside to ask about the enciphering machine. He was most insistent. I answered saying that I was working on it in the workshop of my Malibu ranch home. He wanted to see the workshop at my ranch home but I told him I was far too busy with the projects at the plant to go to the ranch.

I told Kline that during the start-up stage of new projects, I usually stayed close to the plant. I had a small apartment in town I used to sleep and bathe. I also said I might not get to the ranch for weeks at a time. Distressed by this Kline said he wanted to see all progress on the machine. He now expected to have all of the drawings that were associated with his projects along with a weekly report from me.

My reply to Kline was that we had agreed that there would not be a time limit placed on the enciphering machine. I informed him that all drawings are proprietary. Kline went red with anger and said he is not a man to trifle with.

I tried to defuse the moment; I assured Kline that his project had priority over the other engines we were building. He noticed the employees had gathered outside the door, curious about the angry voices. He put his arm around my shoulder to tell me he was sorry for his outburst. Kline said he was under a great deal of pressure. His intercepted communications with the field offices in the different countries resulted in lost sales. He said he dared not to send any formula or manufacturing techniques by wire. He had to send a messenger by ship to hand carry confidential information. He said he could not do that with sales, because it takes too long.

THE ARTIMUS BOX

Some weeks after the Kline visit, I was able to go to the ranch for a weekend. My wife and children were happy to see me. I was often away from my family for weeks at a time. When we have time, I have parties at the ranch for my employees and the racing fraternity.

We have lots of people come to the ranch to relax, eat, drink, and trade ideas and stories. This bench racing is an enjoyable respite from the pressures of work for everyone.

My home workshop is off-limits on these occasions. However, after Kline's visit on that weekend's get together, I found things out of place in the workshop.

Someone had gone through my files and had not returned them in order. Some of the items on shelves were out of place. I had locks put on the doors and windows.

Before I returned to L.A., I was able to do some preliminary work on the enciphering machine. The idea I was pursuing was the use of rotary wheels, much like engine camshafts that change or amplify a motion. The rotary wheels were a strong beginning to change characters.

On my return to the plant, I received a telephone call from my friend, George Stall of the police force. He told me that the information he had gathered about Kline was sketchy. What he had found was that Kline was a member of a political party in Germany.

The Nazi party, already powerful, was gaining members and even more strength. He said Kline was known to be a tough businessman, not above using any method to get what he wanted.

Kline's business interests took him worldwide. My police friend found that Scotland Yard in England had a file on Kline they would not share with him. Kline, as far as my police friend could find, did not have a criminal record.

German politics is not a subject I know about. My father came from Germany but did not subject me to a great deal of German history or heritage. As a child, we never spoke German at home and I have only thought of myself as an American. I have seen this Hitler character on newsreels in the theater. I thought him to be an overblown man, much too full of his own visions. His screaming to the crowds does however seem to stir the people's emotions a great deal.

The V 16-cylinder engine for Kline's car was coming together. I had a new type of crankcase cast in San Francisco. My staff here was finishing the rest of the parts. We would begin dynamometer testing the engine very soon. The frame for the car was being hand hammered from my latest steel alloy. The suspension and driveline parts were drawn and being fabricated.

Supercharged and four wheel drive, this could be the future.

Manley stops reading and stares into the distance. His hands tremble holding the paper. The death of his friend forgotten, he dreams of how he will use the papers to increase his wealth and importance. He gets up from his desk and goes to the bathroom to wash his face and hands. Manley returns to his desk and takes a bottle of scotch from a drawer. He splashes a healthy shot into a glass and sits down to continue reading the journal.

Chapter 15

I telephoned Kline's hotel to invite him to a dyno test of his engine. The person who answered the phone in his room informed me that Mr. Kline was in Brazil on business and would not return for two weeks. I later received a telegram from Kline in which he said his company called him away to Germany. He would be returning to Los Angeles after some delay in time.

Our workload at the plant had diminished due to the depression in the economy. This gave me chance to spend more time at the ranch with my family. I was also able use this time to work on the enciphering machine. I had the machinist at the plant make some rotary wheels and shafts from my hand drawn sketches. I fitted these parts to the machine at my home workshop. This enabled me to visualize how I am going to be able to make this machine function.

At the plant in L.A., we had finished the dynamometer testing on the 300 cubic inch Supercharged V16 with excellent result. The engine was very flexible and made good torque and power.

I was pleased with the finish of the engine and its performance. The very delicate intercooling manifold was beautiful and worked well. Intercooling is one of the keys to producing better horsepower.

Kline returned to L.A. and came to the plant unannounced. He was quite brusque and wanted an in-depth report on his project. He had three men with him and demanded that I accompany them to his club to give him a report.

This melodrama surprised me. I sensed something had changed. Going away with Kline and his men did not make me comfortable. I asked Kline to give me a minute with my shop manager. I said I needed to give him some instruction on the day's work. I informed Fred, my shop manager, that Kline was demanding I go with him to his club. I instructed Fred to alert George, our police friend, that if I did not call Fred or return in an hour to have the police come to Kline's club on La Brea. Fred was alarmed. I tried to assure him that all would be well if he followed my instruction.

In Kline's car on the way to his club, he declared to me that he was under even greater pressure from his board members in Germany. He was to present them with the enciphering machine on his return to Germany. Even though I was concerned with Kline's manner and demands, I reminded him that our agreement precluded a time limit on the enciphering machine.

Kline declared he did not give a damn about the agreement. Moreover, that he was going to take the enciphering machine with him to Germany, along with the completed car and all pertinent drawings. He said the board members sent the men with him to ensure I comply with his demands.

I was hustled from the car into Kline's club by his henchmen. They pushed me down in a chair. For some

THE ARTIMUS BOX

time the men talked amongst themselves. Kline was shouting at them in rapid fire German. One of the men challenged Kline by talking back to him. Kline slapped his face and the other men quickly grabbed the challenger to hold him back.

I informed Kline his manner and demands were ridiculous. I would not comply, and that in America, we abide by the law. In this case, the contract we had states the due date of the completed car, which I could meet. I also reminded him of the verbal agreement we had as to the enciphering machine.

Kline exploded into anger. He shouted that if I cannot deliver his goods he would demand I return all his money immediately. I told Kline he could have his money and that I would destroy the car and the enciphering machine.

Kline said I was a fool and warned that I would not be allowed to destroy anything, his men would see to that. He said the men would take charge of me and not let me out of their sight. To further his point Kline pounded his fist on a table. He seemed to be putting on a show of strength for his men.

At this turn of events, I informed Kline that I must telephone the plant to give them an agreed signal not to bring in the police. I would only do so if I were able to return to the plant unhindered immediately.

Kline laughed. He ordered his men to take me to his warehouse and keep me under guard until he got his property. As Kline's men pulled me out of my chair, there was a commotion outside the door. I could hear the police asking about me. I shouted out, the door of the room banged open, and police officers flooded through.

Kline and his men shrank away from me as my police friend George Stall approached. George, who was in charge of the policemen, wanted to know what was going on. I looked at Kline and said that we had a misunderstanding, that I did not think we needed to have any further trouble over it. However, I did ask my friend to have a good look at Kline and his men in case of any future difficulties. George looked at the men, then asked to see identification from each of them.

Kline protested that he was a German citizen, but George pointed out to Kline, that unless he was a German diplomat, we were in America and that he was the authority here.

Kline and his men turned over their identifications and George declared he would return the papers to them after he checked with headquarters for any wants and warrants on their identities.

I returned to the plant in a black mood and went directly to Fred, my shop manager, to order the destruction of the Kline car and engine. Fred pleaded with me not to destroy the car and engine, but I was adamant that we destroy the car.

I must say Fred surprised me. His argument against my wishes was powerful and moving. We had never had a real argument between us. The substance of his concern was for the staff. Fred knew if I returned the money to Kline and demolished the car and engine, the staff would be the ones to suffer.

In the past, if a customer was not satisfied or if we damaged an engine in dynamometer testing, I would return their money or replace the engine at no charge. This had resulted, at times, in not having the funds to make the payroll. My crew had been fiercely loyal but, as Fred pointed out, the depression was on and that we must pay them. We would surely have to let some men go if we lost everything from the Kline car.

Fred also pointed out that if we removed the supercharger and changed the camshafts in the engine, we could run the car in the Indianapolis race in the spring. Fred told me that he knew of a company that would buy the car. Although I wanted to have my way, Fred was absolutely right. I did need to think of the men working for me.

I telephoned Kline at his hotel to let him know I would be sending his money back for the car. Kline's response was again angry and threatening; he wanted the car and the enciphering machine. I replied that the car was gone and that the machine would be finished when I could. I said I would return his diamonds with the machine, less the expense I had incurred thus far.

I had told Fred about the diamonds and he was again adamant that we look out for ourselves as regard to costs. I must say I was still outraged at Kline for his threats and behavior, so I decided I would keep a few of the diamonds.

Some days later my police friend George called to say a fellow at Scotland Yard had contacted him. The man wanted information about Kline and the three men with him. George sent the man copies of the papers he had taken from Kline and his men. The English policeman telephoned George to ask if the L.A. police could keep an eye on Kline's people for him and keep him informed of their movements.

George said the Scotland Yard man had shared some information about Kline, that the English knew

Kline to be a Nazi agent. I knew then why I had been so troubled working for Kline.

I thought about the supercharger he had inspected in the dynamometer room. The Nazi's could use this engineering for their aircraft engines. My superchargers were making the highest engine boost pressures anyone had seen. This is just what fighter aircraft need for speed and altitude.

I knew someone could use the enciphering machine against America and I would not be a part of that. I then became determined to make the machine nothing but a joke and return it to Kline. I brought the machine from the ranch into the plant to finish my joke on Kline.

I would not build the machine that I envisioned. Kline's machine would not have any real function. The wheels would rotate when the keys were depressed. The shafts would turn, but this action would have no effect. The rotation of the wheels would not transmit any information. I made the rotation move other components within the mechanism and placed some electrical sockets on the floor plate. I placed the remaining diamonds in a hollow shaft of the mechanism and capped the ends of the shaft.

It will take some detailed inspection before Kline finds his diamonds. When he does find them, he will know the joke. Hide your real intentions with lies and threats and what you will get from me in return is this slap in the face.

The journal abruptly ends.

THE ARTIMUS BOX

Chapter 16

Manley has no idea where the Artimus box is now. There are no clues in the journal and as far as he knows, the box has not surfaced. He knows he has to get Dutch the money for the collection and tell him something to keep him from murdering his family. Manley is thinking there could be a clue to the box in the Kim Derby collection.

The Southern California morning breaks with a hazy burnt orange sky. Monday comes too soon. It is a day Manley fears; he has not been able to get much sleep over the weekend. He does not have the money Dutch has demanded; the only way out is to use the deposits from his customers' restoration projects to augment his savings account. For Manley, the threats from Dutch, and the potential of his highly regarded business falling into scandal and ruin now compound his fears.

After leaving the bank, Manley heads for his shop, trying to convince himself that he is in control. He has no real plan; he must rid himself of Dutch, but how?

As Manley turns into his shop entrance, he sees Dutch and his gang massed in his parking lot. These guys are a rough looking group. Manley sees that none of his regular customers has dared to come into the lot. His employees are not visible outside the business.

This is just the way Manley feared the day would begin. Just having Dutch and his gang take up the parking lot would scare most of his customers away. As Manley parks his car, his door opens and he looks up to the evil smirk on Dutch's face.

"You got my dough, glamour boy?"

"Yes Dutch, I have a cashiers check for you."

"What? I want cash. I gotta kick your ass to smarten you up boy?"

"Listen Dutch, I can't get that kind of cash out of the bank without raising a lot of questions. This way no one will care. This is for your protection too."

Manley is fearful that Dutch might not accept the check. His motive for the check is to protect him from an audit if he cannot replace a customer's deposit.

"My protection? You think I need protection from you?"

"Dutch, we need to be careful. The only trail this check leaves is for you as an outside vender for services rendered. It's a lot of money."

"Okay Manley. I'll do it your way but don't ever try that again without my okay first. Here's your stuff, you can keep the van. Now where's the box, man? I want them diamonds. You sell 'em and we'll split the dough."

"I don't know where the box is Dutch. Let me look through the stuff you brought me. Maybe there's a clue to where the box is or who might have it."

"You better be straight with me, glamour boy, or I'll carve you up and feed you to the fish. You try to

THE ARTIMUS BOX

sell those diamonds and don't split with me, I'll slit your old lady's throat, you got that?"

"I know you're a tough guy Dutch. I'm not going to try to screw you. You don't have to threaten me every time you see me. I've got the message. We are in this together. As soon as I know anything about the Artimus box, you will too. I will call you. I will call when I find the answer, but please don't come here. This only makes matters worse. The more people see us together the more questions will be asked."

"You think I care man? Nobody screws with me. I'm the king man. I rule your sorry ass, you best remember that."

"Dutch, when you are here with your whole group, it looks out of place. It means people will tie us together. It means I can't use the Artimus stuff you got because collectors will know it was stolen.

That will mean unless there is a solid clue to where the box is, I can't show that collection. I won't be able to use it to get any of the other Artimus experts to help us find the box."

"Well, glamour boy, you better find that box and quick. You look through that junk in the van and call me."

Dutch gets on his motorcycle, the engines rev with an ear-wracking roar. He and his gang file out of Manley's lot. The thunderous howl of the twenty-some motorcycles shakes the ground as they head for the freeway.

Manley is eager to see the treasures in the van. He is not yet willing to face what the cost is to his family, his business, or that he has caused the death of a friend. He did not think hiring some thugs to keep an eye on his friend Kim Derby would have resulted in a death, or the fears he has to deal with now.

He knew his greed had overshadowed any vestige of his integrity. Manley shakes his head. No, no, no, this is not his fault, he thinks, he has enough problems, and this is all because of Dutch.

He has dealt with the devil, and will have to pay the dues.

THE ARTIMUS BOX

Chapter 17

Manley takes the van with the stolen Artimus collection to a storage unit in Downey. He rents a space, drives the van inside, and closes the pull down door before opening the back of the van. The van is a treasure trove; it will take weeks to go through all of the items. Manley wants to take his time to savor every book. He relishes the thought of every picture, and every piece of memorabilia.

He takes the lid off a cardboard box filled with file folders. The files are marked and alphabetized, and he sees a name, Malcolm Donner, that jumps out at him. Manley knows Donner from the classic car restoration gatherings they have attended. For years, he has envied Donner' extensive Artimus collection. As he looks through the file, he thinks if anyone knows where the Artimus box is, that person would be Donner.

Manley is confident that he and Dutch are the only persons alive that know the real secrets of the Artimus box. He needs to find out what Donner might know of the box, but without raising any suspicion. Manley just wants to get lost in the marvels of the Artimus collection laid out before him. He decides his troubles can wait. He can worry later.

Dutch, however, is not willing to let time go by. Days have passed since he delivered the stolen goods to Manley. Dutch is not a patient guy. He thinks Phil might be trying to screw him. Maybe Phil thinks he can get the diamonds for himself. His paranoia grows each day he does not hear from Phil Manley. Dutch wants the diamonds and he is not about to share the money with Manley. When he finds the box, he will no longer need Manley.

Dutch phones Manley demanding to know where the box is. Manley says there is not any information in the Artimus collection Dutch brought him. Dutch wonders again if Manley is trying to screw him. He wants the box now. He warns Manley not to try to screw with him and to get him the box immediately.

Manley says the only lead he has is a man named Donner. He is the only other source he knows of that might have any more information about the box.

Dutch demands to know how to find Donner.

Manley shudders at his mistake. He does not want Dutch to tip Donner off or to rough him up. Manley suggests to Dutch that he will talk to Donner to see if he knows anything. He says they must be careful not to let anyone know the secrets they have about the box. Manley says that Donner has a huge Artimus collection and in that collection may rest the secret they are looking for to find the box.

Dutch screams at Manley. "I'll do what I want asshole, you don't tell me how to do nothin'. I know how to get the stuff we need, all you have to do is tell me where I can find Donner."

Manley reluctantly gives Dutch, Donner's Santa Monica address.

THE ARTIMUS BOX

"Come on Dutch. You're holding all the cards. I won't try anything, but Donner has extensive connections in the car collection world and that it would be a mistake to confront him. Besides, if Donner finds out about the box he might be able to locate it before we can. If we even make him suspicious, he could foul up the whole deal. The man knows everyone with any Artimus pieces. I'm just saying take it easy, that's all."

Dutch just leers at Manley. "All I care about's the dude's local man."

He did not know how he would deal with Donner if Donner were located outside of the state or country. Now Dutch knows he can use his whole gang to get the box or the information to lead him to it.

At the Santa Monica City Hall, Dutch searches through the property records to find information on the Donner property.

He finds that Donner bought all of the bungalows on the west side of a courtyard. The bungalows were originally built as single-family units in 1930; Donner had the entire east side remodeled into one large residence. The remodeling project also joined the attached garages together into one large space.

Dutch jumps on his motorcycle to reconnoiter the Donner place and the surrounding area. As he rides around the quiet residential neighborhood, he sees that the people living in the area are curious about the racket his motorcycle makes. They draw back their curtains and some even come out of their homes to shake their fists in disgust at Dutch for the outrageous noise his big V twin makes.

Dutch reasons that he needs to continue his surveillance in something more discreet. He knows trying to break into Donner' house from the front entrance will be very risky; he needs to find another way in. Dutch returns the next day in a rental car and quietly tours the Donner neighborhood again. He finds an alleyway behind the bungalows and notes that the attached garages behind the Donner home still have the old-time double wooden swing out doors. He has found his way in, the center set of doors have only one old dead bolt lock to secure them. Dutch can now send one of his men to watch the place to determine the best time to break in.

Four days later, Dutch's man reports that Donner has just left his house in a taxicab with a travel bag and a suitcase. The man informs Dutch that the courtyard complex is a working neighborhood and is mostly vacant from 7am to 5pm.

Dutch assembles his three best men to plan the break-in details. The plan is to break into the house through the garage at 3am and lay low in the house until after daybreak. Then after making sure the people of the courtyard complex have left for the day, they will search the Donner home for the Artimus box or for some clue to its whereabouts. Dutch figures they can find the box, steal any valuables they want and be out of the place by noon. They will make their exit by the garage.

The four men steal a van in Lancaster, change the license plates and drive to Santa Monica. At 3 am, they park the van near the mouth of the alleyway and post one man as a lookout. The remaining three men proceed to the garage. One man carries a large crowbar; the other two men have furniture blankets to deaden sound, and backpacks for the stolen loot.

The men go to the center doors and the man with the crowbar shoves the end of the bar between the doors under the dead bolt lock. The two other men place the heavy blankets around the lock and the crowbar. There is a muted crack as the wood splinters away from the lock. The doors swing free and the men enter the darkness of the Donner garage. After securing the broken doors behind them, Dutch turns on his flashlight to locate the door to the interior of the house. The beam of the flashlight reflects off the highly polished surfaces of the early American racing cars Donner has stored in his garage.

Dutch grins to himself as the ray of his flashlight finds a door to the home's interior. The door does not even have a lock, just a simple doorknob. He figures this Donner character is a fool.

Dutch opens the door and steps into a beautifully remodeled kitchen. Even in the darkness of the room, you can make out the gleaming surfaces of the latest appliances. This Donner is a rich fool, he thinks. There should be plenty of valuable stuff to steal; this is going to be easy pickings.

The other two men with Dutch come into the kitchen and go straight to the refrigerator. One yanks the door open, and its light floods the room.

Dutch slaps at the man. "Hey you simple shit, turn off that Goddamn light!"

There is a window to the outside, as well as a sky light in the ceiling of the kitchen that will give off light that can be seen from outside.

"You dudes keep quiet and find somewhere to roost till sun up."

As the sun filters into the Donner house, Dutch begins the search for the Artimus box. The search is not a gentle one. In the study, Dutch pulls books from the shelves and after thumbing through them, and dumps them on the floor. He can hear his men ransacking the other rooms of the house.

Dutch finds a large leather-bound book. In it are drawings of various racing car engines and parts. He goes through the pages and finds a drawing of the type of mechanism he remembers from the papers he took from Kim Derby. Dutch puts the book in his backpack and continues his search.

At 9 a.m., Dutch hears singing as someone walks into the courtyard and approaches the Donner house. He runs into the living room of the house to find his men.

"You guys shut up and get the hell in the kitchen, we got company."

The men can hear the front door locks opening. Dutch whispers, "Stay here I'll go see who it is." He creeps toward the foyer.

Malcolm Donner's housekeeper of many years opens the front door. Singing to herself, she enters the room and turns on the lights. She heads to the supply closet to get the cleaning supplies to begin her day when she suddenly stops. The room is a mess, the foyer table is overturned, the umbrella stand is lying on the floor with the umbrellas scattered.

Dutch starts around the corner of the room to make a grab for the housekeeper. The woman catches flash of movement and screams at the top of her lungs. She

THE ARTIMUS BOX

turns around and runs out of the front door. She runs down the courtyard yelling "Help, Police! Help, Police!"

Dutch goes back to the study to grab his backpack, picks it up and runs toward the back of the house to collect the other men. They scrabble to get out of the house. The men burst out of the garage, and run down the alley to the stolen van.

His lookout, slumped over the steering wheel, jolts awake as Dutch jerks open the rear door of the van. Dutch charges to the front of the van, punches the driver in the face, picks up a tire iron and starts beating the man.

Dutch's men try to stop him. One man grabs the tire iron away from Dutch, and the other man puts his arms around Dutch to trap his flailing arms. The man with the tire iron yells at Dutch. He says they have to get away before the cops show up.

Dutch stops struggling, he grabs the tire iron back from the one man and orders him to get the van started and get them out of there. After they get clear of the area, Dutch tells the battered lookout man that he is going to kill him for letting the housekeeper surprise them. His face is contorted and red; the veins in his neck stand out. He turns to the man that tried to stop him from beating the lookout. Dutch screams, "The next time you touch me, you asshole, I'll tear your arms off and beat you to death with 'em."

Dutch beats on the interior of the van with the tire iron. The two men in the back shrink away trying to keep out of his reach. The driver keeps looking over his shoulder as the van careens down the road. All that stuff in the Donner house is worth a fortune Dutch thinks. He did not find the Artimus box, and that damned housekeeper got away. He would have to go back. He would wait for the police to finish their robbery investigations and then go back, and this time he would to do it right.

Now he wanted to vent. First, he would kill the man that caused him to lose the loot. The killing would be as slow and painful as his rage would allow.

The trip to the desert to bury the man would be a cooling off period for him. Keeping his gang fearful of him was one job Dutch enjoyed; let them see a weak spot and they would tear it open.

After a trip to the desert to dispose of the body, and get rid of the stolen van, Dutch decides the next thing on his list is to make Manley find the box. He has the book he took from Donner's house, maybe the clue would be in the drawings.

He will make copies of the book and then sell it to Manley. Dutch will make Manley's life hell on earth until he finds him the box. He enjoys the torture he inflicts on Manley, the jerk is so easy to scare. The fear and pain on his face every time he sees Dutch, makes him laugh. It is like a drug high for Dutch, he is all-powerful, so in control, and so much smarter than anyone else. He can stare anyone down; he can bend anyone to his will. He is invincible, the strongest, toughest son of a bitch alive.

THE ARTIMUS BOX

Chapter 18

Manley reads in the paper that Malcolm Donner has had a break-in at his home. The newspaper article states that no one was home when the break-in occurred. The housekeeper discovered the break-in upon entering the home. She found the furniture in the foyer in disarray and thought someone was still there. This caused her to run from the home screaming for the police. The article also has a description of the items stolen and a statement from Donner.

The newspaper quotes Donner as saying that he has lived in the neighborhood for over twenty years, and had never experienced any problems. This had led him to a false sense of security. He had been very lax in providing the security measures that his home needed to have. He went on to say that a state of the art security system was being installed, and that it will not only protect from break-ins, but the system will also contain a fire suppression system throughout the house and garages. The systems will have a connection to the local police and fire departments.

Manley feels relieved that Donner and his housekeeper were unharmed. He knows Dutch will be back, barking in his face with more threats of violence.

He needs to make a plan to get rid of Dutch before his life is ruined.

As sure as sunrise, Dutch shows up at Manley's shop the next day. He comes into Manley's office with a paper bag and slaps it down on his desk. "Open the bag old buddy."

Manley looks up at Dutch, and cautiously opens the bag. In it, he finds the leather bound book from the Donner break-in.

"This is from Donner's?"

"That's right buddy boy, go ahead open it."

The book is magnificent. Inside are the treasured drawings. They are each works of fine art. The pieces drawn are some of the finest automotive engineering of early American racing. Manley cannot take his eyes from the book, he turns each page with a child's anticipation.

Manley hates and fears Dutch, but the Artimus collection he has brought would never have been available to him without Dutch getting it for him. Manley is lost in the book of drawings. Dutch watches Manley's face, then angrily growls at him, "I want ten thousand for the book, man."

Manley's mind snaps back into the present, a muscle in his cheek ticks. "Dutch I don't have another ten thousand to give you. I gave you all the money I can come up with right now. You must have looked through this book. Did you see anything in it that tells us where the box is?"

"How the hell do I know Manley? I want the diamonds and I want 'em now. I'm putting it to you to come up with a way to find the box or the diamonds. I

THE ARTIMUS BOX

don't care how you do it but do it quick. Keep the book. I'll be back to collect for it later."

"Dutch we may never find the box. The diamonds could have been lost or sold decades ago. We may never know. I've read articles about the mysteries of the Artimus box, but as far as I know, no one alive today has ever seen it, or knows where it might be. The whole story is over sixty years old."

"I don't want to hear that crap Manley. Just look through all the stuff I got for you and find an answer. I want the dough. I got some big deals going and I need the jack. I ain't spend'n much more time on you, every time I see you pisses me off. You're a worm. You ain't got no back bone." Dutch slams the door behind him as he storms out of Manley's office.

Manley shuts down the shop and goes to his storage unit to examine the book and the rest of his treasures. He has outfitted his unit with office furniture, a wine rack and a small refrigerator to store exotic cheeses. He spends many hours alone enjoying his Artimus collection. No one knows of his secret hiding place. He can get away from Dutch and the worries over the money he took from the business to pay Dutch.

He does try hard to find some clue as to the whereabouts of the box. However, he can find nothing in the collection he has that will help him. Manley is smart enough to know that if he ever did find the box it would never satisfy Dutch.

Dutch becomes a regular visitor to Manley's shop. He is always threatening, always abusive. He is sure Manley is trying to screw him. He tells Manley he needs money and he means big money. He says he has big deals going. Year after year Dutch is all over

Manley. Year after year Manley finds himself smothered by self-loathing, his life shattered. Dutch is gone for a month or two only to show up at Manley's shop or home demanding money. Each time Dutch disappears Manley hopes in vain that he has gone for good. Again, Dutch does not show up at Manley's, but this time it is for months. The terrible cycle that is tearing him apart repeats.

It has been almost a year since Dutch made his last visit. Manley hopes Dutch is gone for good, maybe one of his deals went bad, or better yet, maybe someone did the world a favor and killed him. Manley tries to find out what has happened to Dutch. He has come across one of the members of Dutch's gang that he recognizes in the Old Towne Mall parking lot.

Manley asks the man where Dutch is. The man tells him that Dutch went to Mexico for some deal and the last he heard Dutch was in Columbia. "Do you have any idea when he's coming back?"

The man spits a glob of black tobacco juice at Manley's feet. "He'll be back when he wants to be. You don't need to know nothin' more man. Don't stick your nose in where it's gonna get chopped off. You get me dude?"

The years of fear have taken their toll on Manley. His stomach churns and his bowels are a constant worry; he has lost weight and his complexion is pasty white. The suspense of not knowing when Dutch may show up, or what threats he will have to endure keeps Manley sleepless.

Months go by and no Dutch. Manley is putting his life back together. He is able to put back a good deal of the money that he took out of the business to pay

THE ARTIMUS BOX

Dutch. He managed to put enough money into the proper accounts to finish the customers' cars. Manley begins to gain back some of the weight he lost. He wants to believe the nightmare is over. Phil dreams of the day he can introduce the Artimus collection as his own.

Manley is in his shop on a Saturday admiring the finish work one of his vendors completed on a sculpted hood ornament. The coolness of the chromed form of a winged angel in his hand is somehow soothing. The spell is broken when he hears the dreaded roar of Dutch's motorcycle. Phil wants to believe it cannot be true, but no, the devil himself struts through the front door. He takes long quick strides to stand nose to nose with a shaken Manley.

"Alright asshole, I need big dough fast," snarls Dutch. "Get it for me now!"

Manley takes a step back. "I, I don't have any more money man," he stammers. "Look just give me a break, business is bad. I need a break Dutch; I need some time to get things together."

"Yeah I'll give you a break alright. You never paid me for the book, man."

As Manley tries to back away, Dutch stays in his face. "I need dough fast," he snarls, "I had a little trouble with my Columbian pals. I got some big deals goin' but I gotta have dough right now. You owe me. The only break you get is to live long enough to pay me off. Quit shakin' little man and get my dough."

Dutch stalks through Manley's shop, then stops at one of the stalls where a Boat-Tail Auburn is having the final touches done. The car is a giant by today's standards and Manley's staff has beautifully restored it. It gleams in the well-lighted shop.

Dutch turns to Manley. "Hey man who owns this baby?"

"It belongs to a man that lives in upper New York State."

"No that ain't no good to me man." He yanks Manley by the arm and drags him roughly into the office. In the office, Dutch closes the door and pounds on a file cabinet. "How many guys you got that live somewhere close?"

"You know, I just got me the idea of where I'm goin' to get some big dough man.

You're gonna' get me the names and addresses of your richest clients and I'm goin' to pay them a midnight visit. Hell, these chumps gotta have millions to throw away and I'm just the dude to get it from 'em."

"Come on Dutch, I can't be involved in that kind of thing. These people trust me."

"Man you ain't got any choices in this. You pony up the names or I go to the papers with the Derby story. You're gonna do what I tell you man. I can ruin you or I can kill you. You're ass is mine, you remember that. Now get me a name. We'll start with one and see how it pans out."

Manley staggers forward, then doubles over, and throws up over his desk. Dutch grabs Manley by the shirt collar. He drags him to a bank of file cabinets.

"Get me a name, you candy ass. You wussys just piss me off. You wanted that Artimus stuff and didn't care how you got it. Now you're gonna to play along and like it. Get me that book, too, man. I'm gonna sell it."

THE ARTIMUS BOX

Manley wipes his face and unrolls paper towels to mop up his desk. Beads of sweat cover his face. His hands shake and after disposing of the soiled towels, he looks very pale. Phil sits down behind his desk and looks up at Dutch.

Manley buries his head in a large handkerchief coughs and blows his nose. "I don't have the book here Dutch; I'll bring it in tomorrow. I'll get you the name you want. But if you sell the book, the person that buys it will know it's been stolen and that will come right back on us."

"No way man. I gotta guy can sell it, and ain't nobody gonna to know where it comes from."

Manley is right back in it again. He brings his appointment book and goes through it to give Dutch the name of one of his clients who has a very large art and coin collection as well as classic cars.

Dutch says "Don't worry, old buddy I ain't gonna kill no one if I don't have to. I'll be back soon."

Left with a foul taste in his mouth and his stomach in a knot, Manley gets a milk carton from small office refrigerator and takes a tentative sip. He sits down at his desk; the stench of his own vomit is revolting. He gets up and walks out of the room as he hears Dutch's bike roaring off in the distance. His stomach be damned, he goes back in the office and pulls open a desk drawer. He grabs a bottle of scotch and twists the cap off. The cap goes skipping across the room.

Putting the bottle to his mouth, he takes a long pull. Maybe this is the answer, stay drunk, or drink enough to die from it. That is the only protection from Dutch he can find.

In three weeks Dutch returns, "Man what a haul. That dude's got more stuff than I got time to steal. I fenced all that stuff in no time too. Get me another name man. I'm back to dealin' big time. This is easy money."

As more years go by Dutch wants more names, and Manley's depression is growing deeper. His wife has divorced him and taken their children, along with his grand house. He is becoming an alcoholic; this coupled with a decline in his personal hygiene, finds his friends shunning him. He spends more time shut away in the tiny storage unit with his precious collection. His business is going down hill. His clients have seen the change in Manley also. Soon his employees are leaving to join shops that are more prestigious.

Dutch has ruined him; he has become mired in self-hate. If only he could get rid of Dutch, if only he could stand up to Dutch.

Dutch, too, is going downhill. His use of drugs and steroids has taken their toll. It makes him feel invincible, his gang members are amazed when his 'roid rages take him. He seems completely out of control. He is dangerous to anyone around him. Only the few men that have been with Dutch from the beginning, and are doing the same drugs, stay by him.

The ten years since the murder of Kim Derby and the start of the quest for the Artimus box has caused ruined lives and dangerous frustrations for Dutch and his gang. Dutch gets word from his police informant that the Artimus box has come to light. It is evidence in a 1932 murder case. Manley was telling the truth all these years. Dutch wants the box now more than ever. He feels he has a lot invested.

THE ARTIMUS BOX

One small-time cop is all that stands in his way.

Chapter 19

Van is up early on Saturday and ready to start the day. He watches Formula One qualifying on TV, and makes breakfast for Kathy and himself. After breakfast, Van calls Donner to see if they can meet. Donner answers the phone seated in his armchair wearing a smoking jacket. He is enjoying coffee made with freshly ground beans from his French press coffee maker. The aroma fills the room and is as delicious as the coffee itself.

"Yes by all means please do come to my house. I am eager to show you the results of my research. I have found some very interesting records that I never knew existed."

Van gives a thumbs up to Kathy who is standing close by. "Thank you that sounds fantastic. I wonder if you might have time to show me your car collection."

"My cars are my pride and joy. I would be delighted to show them to you. If you have time to stay for lunch we can go through my research and I can give you the nickel tour."

Van replies that would be nice and that he would like to bring Kathy with him. Donner says he would be delighted to see her also.

THE ARTIMUS BOX

They arrive at Donner's house and ring the doorbell. Donner answers the door, "It is a pleasure to meet you Mr. Taylor. Kathy has told me so much about you."

"Please, call me Van."

"Yes, very good. Please do the same for me, my name is Malcolm." With the formal greetings concluded, Malcolm shows them into his study.

The room, the books, and all the racing mementos Donner has collected, dazzle Van. He wants to see and touch everything like a little kid. Donner is a very kind host and is willing to allow some of his pieces to be touched and to tell the story behind every piece and every book. He is very patient and willing to let Van roam around the room. Finally Van realizes he has taken up a good deal of time just looking at various items and asking Donner questions.

Kathy smiles at Van and says to Donner, "He's like a kid in a candy store, Malcolm. We don't want to take up your whole day."

Van, having forgotten the time also, apologizes to Donner.

"This room is marvelous, Malcolm, it must have taken you decades to collect these pieces and to display them so well. I'm sorry, I just lost myself and all track of time."

"Not to worry. A pleasure of owning such a collection is to see the enjoyment it brings to others. I do allow some other serious collectors to use the books as reference material. I have meetings here with my colleagues to discuss new finds and trade information. If you're ready we can go into the dining room and have a luncheon I have prepared for us."

Donner shows them into the elegant dining room and seats them at the table. He excuses himself to go to the kitchen to bring out the food.

In the middle of the large linen-covered table is a multi-tiered mahogany wood lazy Susan. On the tiers, there are small glass bowls of pickles, carrots, chopped onion, and many varieties of sauces. The places are set with good china, sterling silver and cut crystal glassware. Kathy and Van exchange looks of raised eyebrows.

"Wow, this is some spread," Van says, "maybe I should have worn my tux."

Donner returns from his kitchen with a platter of hot dogs and hamburgers.

He puts down the platter and returns to the kitchen only to come back with more platters of corn on the cob and salads. Donner smiles impishly at the surprise he sees in the eyes of his guests. "I like to cook for myself on occasion, but I have never learned to make the finer gourmet plates. I hope this will suffice."

Van and Kathy roar with laughter, and an obviously fun-loving Donner joins in. With the ice broken, the formality gone, they dig into the food. The three of them recount stories of their own racing adventures while feasting on the hot dogs and hamburgers piled high with the contents of the lazy Susan.

Donner has brought in a silver ice bucket with chilled champagne. After the feast, they push their chairs back from the table and Kathy rises to say that she will help with the dishes. Donner will not hear of it.

"I will take the dishes and dinnerware to the kitchen. I have a commercial type dishwashing machine

THE ARTIMUS BOX

to keep them in until my housekeeper can deal with them. It's the only way I can keep house."

Donner removes the dishes, and Kathy helps to clean the table of the remainder of a memorable meal. They all return to the study and Donner has them seated in large red leather armchairs facing a wall-mounted plasma screen as he begins to display his latest research.

"I am very anxious to know what you can tell me about the box you found with the body of Tim Wahl. As you know, I am an avid collector of Harry Artimus artifacts. The Artimus box has been a myth for more than seventy years. Now that the box has actually been found it is of the greatest importance to me."

"Malcolm, my Captain's ordered me not to give out any information about the box. You've been attacked and so have I. The fewer people that know about the box, the better chance we have of discovering the bad guys. I've brought you some pictures of the box, and I promise that you'll be the first to know of any new developments."

"I understand your position, Van. I do appreciate the pictures. This is like opening a Christmas present for me."

Malcolm studies each picture closely. "Can you tell me if it is a working encryption machine?"

"Well, Malcolm, you've been a wonderful host and, if you promise to keep this to yourself, I'll tell you that the machine seems to have been a model or prototype. The machine itself doesn't function other than to revolve the wheels when the keys are pressed."

Donner is studying the pictures with a magnifying glass. "I appreciate you telling me what you can. The pictures are very good; I can see Harry's handiwork in these photos. The fit and finish are what he would have demanded, and the design is elegant as always. I have wanted to see the box for forty years. I will scan these pictures into my computer program and study them at length later. Therefore, in trade, I am hoping that this will help you in your investigation. I have been able to find quite a bit of information about Tim Wahl.

"I had not focused any of my research on the Artimus box to Tim Wahl in the past. It was only after you brought your information to me that I became aware of him. I have gone back to some of my previous interviews with the principles of my Harry Artimus research.

"After the break-in ten years ago I put all of the files I collected in the past forty five years into my computer. I still marvel at the way I can input a name or even a phrase, and the program will locate it from my files. Tim Wahl's name came up in an interview I conducted with Harry's wife in 1958. I was trying to gather information about Harry as a person. I wanted to get a feel of him through the heart and mind of his wife, Mae.

"She was a wonderful lady, and still a very pretty and petite woman in her 60's. She was very devoted to Harry. Harry was very loving and good to Mae; he made sure that she had all of her needs seen to. She survived Harry by almost thirty years, and in fine style. As Mae was talking about Harry, she said he was a very kind, mild-mannered man, and this is where Tim Wahl comes in.

"Mae told me, Harry hired a boy that had been coming to his shop for years just to hang around and look at the cars and talk to the men Harry had working for him.

"Harry put the boy to work by having him sweep the floors to see if he was really interested in working or just wanted to waste time.

"Harry found that the boy was indeed a worker and that the men in the shop liked him. Harry made it a point to show the boy how things worked, and would then give him jobs that would use that knowledge.

"The boy's name was Tim Wahl. He had only worked for Harry a short time when he went missing. Mae related to me that Harry was beside himself. He had very bad feelings about the fate of the boy and felt responsible for Tim.

"She was telling me this because it was one of the few times she had witnessed Harry being angry enough to be cross and irritable. She went on to say that, for a time after the Wahl disappearance, Harry actually carried a pistol with him and came to the ranch every night instead of staying at his apartment in town during the workweek. Harry's behavior badly frightened Mae, she asked Harry what made him so upset.

"Harry told Mae not to worry, that he would keep her safe and that one of his clients was a bad man that he wanted arrested for assaulting a man that worked for him. He promised Mae all would be well. She said it was the only time that she could remember Harry being irritable, and somewhat remote toward her.

"After I found that reference to Wahl, I turned to the newspaper articles of the day to see what I could find."

"I found an article in the L.A. paper about the Wahl disappearance myself," interjects Van.

"I can see that you would Van, but the articles I found led me to others and to Horst Kline who was the client in question. Harry wanted Kline arrested for an assault on Jos Vermane who was one of his employees. I was able to trace Kline by researching any article or mention of him worldwide, from his emergence in the early 1920's to his demise by the Nazi's in 1934.

"The significance of this is the timeline. Harry agrees to build a V16 car for Kline after the Indianapolis 500 race in June of 1931. They have a falling out in late January or early February of 1932 and Tim Wahl disappears that same February. Then Artimus has the original V16 cylinder Kline car converted from the centrifugal supercharger engine to a normally aspirated engine. The car was sold to a participant of the 1932 500 race but the car's performance was disappointing. The reason they took the supercharger off was that the rules governing the 1932 Indianapolis 500 did not allow superchargers.

"The engine, without the supercharger, was not as powerful as it should have been. This was probably due to the little development time Harry had before the race to make it better. What makes that interesting is that the car is one I have in my collection. The records I traced years ago when I purchased the car did not indicate any ownership by Kline.

"I decided to find out all I could about Kline, and if you will bear with me, I think I can shed some light on the Wahl murder.

"Kline first entered the German record keeping machine in 1924; he was put in charge of a large bearing company that was taken over by the Nazis. I cannot find any record of birth for Kline. I think this means that he was an invention by the Nazis to run the bearing company. The German newspapers of the time claim that Kline was a master of industry and had not only increased the production of the company but had expanded the company's holding to become a major worldwide concern.

"The newspaper articles continued the generous reports of Kline's business conquests. The existing German records show that the monies used to expand the bearing company were from government coffers, and not Kline's genius. Kline's rise continued and he was constantly on the move. He visited major manufacturing companies worldwide. He was allowed inside major aircraft and ship building companies in the US and Europe.

"It is obvious now that he was used by the Nazis to gather information on the designs and capabilities of what would become their opposition in World War Two. By the time Kline met Harry Artimus, the Nazi regime had come to full power. Kline is so full of himself he now believed all the glowing press he had been getting over the years. He was very busy collecting information and people that could get him insider information. From the Nazi records I have traced to Kline, he used bribery, blackmail, and coercion to get what he wanted, or what the Nazis wanted.

"I found large sums of money and diamonds given to Kline by the Nazis to use as bribes. One such record is for $150,000.00 to purchase a racing car from Harry Artimus, and an undisclosed number of diamonds for cryptic engineering. This is the first time I have seen that term used, but with what we know now there is no doubt that Kline hired Harry to make an encryption machine.

"It is interesting to note that when I checked the records from Artimus Engine Works for the car Kline commissioned, Harry's records indicate that Kline paid Harry $35,000.00 for the car. The Artimus records also indicate that Harry returned that same sum of money to Kline after their falling out. The Nazi records state that an investigation was launched into Kline's alleged embezzlement of funds.

"In late 1931, he was ordered to send the supercharger drawings made by Artimus Engine Works to his controllers in Germany. In early 1932, Kline's masters ordered him to send them the drawings of the supercharger, and now also the encryption device.

In Kline's reply to his superiors, he stated that Artimus had been uncooperative and refused to give him any drawings or to deliver the encryption machine. He also said that Artimus had kept the money and diamonds he had paid to him and that that amounts to over $250,000.00.

"Kline was ordered to send a full accounting of funds given to him for the previous five years, and to return to Germany immediately to defend himself against allegations of embezzlement of government funds. To make matters worse for Kline, he apparently tried to empty his bank accounts and vanish. The men he thought were under his command stopped him before he could make his escape.

These men were ultimately under the command of Kline's Nazi controllers. The controllers ordered the men to watch Kline for just such an action.

THE ARTIMUS BOX

"Kline was returned to Germany under guard and taken directly to Gestapo headquarters in Berlin. In the interrogation report by the Gestapo, I found that the Gestapo placed Kline in a foul smelling, cold, damp cell and kept him there for days.

"The following is what I have pieced together from the records. I wrote my own report using the records, but I must caution that I have added a few of my own embellishments. Let's first take a break and finish the champagne."

Chapter 20

Donner arranges his notes on an end table and stands behind the table with a pair of half round reading glasses perched on the end of his nose. He clears his throat and begins.

"He was fed stale bread in dark oily water. There was no night and day in the cellblock; there was only a single bright light in the ceiling of his cell with no window to the outside. Kline could hear human screams and heavy boots marching outside of his cell. He was so frightened that he could not sleep or contain himself."

"After three days he was taken to a room and placed in a wooden chair. He had his arms shackled to the chair. His guards left him to wait…his imagination ran wild. Kline waited for what seemed to be hours. He jumped in the chair when the heavy door banged open."

"A very tall blond-haired man entered the room. His posture was of military bearing; his manner was that of complete confidence. He was dressed in an immaculate black uniform with the SS Death's Head insignia on the lapels. Entering the room with the blond man was a very large ugly man. The man's face was scarred, one eye had no eyelid, and he dressed only in a stained leather apron and tall rubber boots."

THE ARTIMUS BOX

"Kline had only heard the gruesome horror tales of torture by the Gestapo. The sight of the second man frightened Kline so badly he wet himself, a dark trail of fetid moisture dripped from the edge of his chair. The tall blond man looked at Kline with utter disgust."

"Kline was suddenly cold and shaking. Before the man in front of him spoke a word, Kline said he would tell him whatever he wanted; he said he would cooperate completely. The tall blond man laughed; he said he knew Kline would cooperate fully. The Gestapo man slapped Kline's face, and said that his friend was there to make sure of it."

"The ugly man's thick lips parted to reveal rotted black teeth as he stepped toward Kline's chair and leaned down to stare into his eyes. Kline tried to turn his head away from the gruesome sight of the man's disfigured face. The ugly man grabbed Kline's head with huge dirty hands to make him face his horror."

Donner reads from his file and alters his voice to bring the different characters to life. He is almost like the comic figure of an English schoolmaster. He is serious and plays the different parts with aplomb. Well into the parts, he gestures and struts as the characters take him. Donner lowers his voice and Van and Kathy lean forward in their seats to hear him.

"The blond man spoke in a low gentle voice. 'You will tell me what I want to know, you will not lie to me. You may address me as Herr Brande. I have a dossier on you that says you are an important person, that you are an asset to Germany. I have orders not to kill you. However, let me make myself perfectly clear. If you lie to me, I will make sure that you will wish to die. Do we have an understanding Herr Kline?

"Yes, yes," croaked Kline, his throat now very dry." Donner's hand goes to his throat; he casts his eyes upward as if he is looking up at his inquisitor. "I am in complete agreement with you. I have only tried to serve the party in the best ways I know. I have brought important information from all over the world. I work only for the party, only for Germany."

"Why do you not have the supercharger drawings and specifications we paid for?" Brande snarled. Donner hunches over the table looking down, his is voice soft but menacing. "Where are the diamonds you were given to procure the enciphering machine? Why did you empty the bank accounts and try to run?"

"I…, I wanted to bring the money back to Berlin to show that I had not embezzled any of the money. I tried to get the car and the machine from Artimus but he tricked me. He kept the money I gave him but refused to complete the work I paid for. I tried to abduct Artimus to force him to comply, but he had the police break in and stop me. I sent my men to get the machine but they failed to get it.

"I sent them to force one of the Artimus employees to steal the drawings but my men failed in this also. They failed and then I was under suspicion by the police. They had a warrant for my arrest. I only just got to the ship before they could arrest me. These events were beyond my control, I am not at fault. The men that were assigned to me are incompetent."

"Why then did you book a passage on a ship bound for Brazil, Herr Kline? Answer me now why?"

"I was, uh, I was trying to mislead the police into thinking I was bound for Brazil."

THE ARTIMUS BOX

"Now I think you are lying. I will leave you with my friend here, while I confer with our superiors."

At this point, Donner stops reading from the notes in front of him. He takes off his glasses and says to Van, "This is the part of the Tim Wahl mystery that we can put to bed so to speak." Donner then continues to read from his notes.

"Herr Brande returned to the room some time later, he barked at Kline that he had a full report from the three men Kline had assigned to him. They reported huge excesses by Kline; also, that he had spent far less money for the information than he reported. As to his failure to retrieve the enciphering machine, their report states that they were deliberately denied the information they needed to retrieve it successfully."

"Their report stated that Kline could not give them a description of the machine or direct them to a course of action. They decided on their own to watch the Artimus shop for anyone leaving with something they thought could be the machine.

"One night in February 1932, they saw a boy leaving the shop late after the other workers had left. They noticed that the lights in the shop had not been turned off by the last man they saw leave before the boy came out, and decided to keep watch on the place. When they spotted the boy with a box, the boy saw them, and ducked behind a corner of a building on the street. After they fired a warning shot to stop him, the boy ran through an alleyway and they gave chase. They lost sight of him for a while, and then one of the men saw the boy with the box under his arm. The moon silhouetted him crouching by a corner beam on a first story platform in a building site. They moved to a position that would afford them a shot at the boy and fired several shots. They all saw the boy fall with the box.

"As they ran to the lot where the boy fell, they saw people were already coming out of some of the neighboring buildings to see what the noise was. The man with the rifle hid it and the rest of the men split up to search the dark lot. They soon found the boy but, before they could take the box, the neighborhood men came into the building site. Kline's men pulled the boy's body out of view to a dirt berm built up around a hole dug alongside a support beam.

"One of the men grabbed the box from the boy's grasp. Just then, a policeman approached them, the beam of his flashlight moving back and forth scanning the lot. The leader of the killers quickly moved toward the cop to distract him. He stepped around the cop to make him turn away from the other men. Hidden from the cop's view, the other men dropped the box and pushed it along with the body into the hole. One of the men kicked dirt from the pile around the hole to cover the body. The policeman asked what they were doing. The leader of the men said, in a thick German accent, that they had heard shots and were looking to see what was going on.

"The policeman turned and ran the beam of his flashlight over the other men. He wanted to know why the man was kicking the dirt. The leader replied that one of the men had just taken a leak there. The policeman walked over and looked at the men, glanced at the dark hole and then told them to go home. He said he would do the investigating.

THE ARTIMUS BOX

"When they cautiously returned to the site the next night, they discovered the whole area around where they had left the boy covered in concrete. A policeman also stood guard at the entrance gate."

Donner shakes his head, "It seems that not only justice is blind."

Chapter 21

"Bravo Malcolm, I am very impressed. Man you can spin a good yarn," exclaims Van. "How in the world did you find such detailed records?"

"Well as you may know, I have been a collector of art and early American auto racing memorabilia for most of my life. During the course of my collections, I have met and been in contact with a great many people who, like me, collect things. These are collectors who are not limited to just automobiles and racing, but they are all men of passion. Passion is the great motivator. The cruelties of war and the inhumanity of man also have a large following. We all tend to stay in contact with each other and we all collaborate with the records we maintain to help with research on a myriad of subjects.

"Some of the work is just simple digging through records. For instance, when I could pinpoint the date of Tim Wahl's shooting, I then went to L.A. building records for the days just before the shooting and just after.

"I found from a county building inspector's concrete sign-off report dated the day after Wahl was murdered, that concrete trucks were brought to the

THE ARTIMUS BOX

building site on Washington Boulevard. They poured base flooring to provide a foundation for the first story structure.

"I am sure the concrete buried poor Tim without anyone other than the killers knowing that he and the Artimus box were there. I was also able to find some newspaper reports of gunshots reported around the Artimus plant and the Washington Boulevard building site on the night of Wahl's murder.

"The record of Kline in Germany was brought to my attention by a colleague of mine in Europe who has been involved with Nazi war criminal investigations. He is also a European automotive expert and has been instrumental in locating some of the Artimus cars that were in Europe and hidden from the Nazis during the war.

"It seems that Kline was involved in some nefarious deals in Brazil before the war and Herr Brande was wanted for war crimes after the war ended.

"The records the Nazis kept were amazing in their detail. The US Army seized mountains of them during and after the war. Private collectors and Israeli intelligence have found even more records. My friend has confirmed to me that the Nazis hanged Horst Kline in 1934 for crimes against the party, and then seized his company and properties.

"After the fall of Berlin, Herr Brande was caught trying to get into Switzerland dressed as a woman. Brande shot himself to death in his cell after an initial interrogation by US Army personnel. Apparently, his jailers missed the pistol Brande had hidden in his belongings.

"Now that we have Wahl's murder cleared up, I suspect you must have some idea of why the Artimus box has brought so much trouble. The box must have another element to it; do you know what it is? Do you want me to keep researching?"

"I have a good idea of the other element as you call it Malcolm, but as I said before I can't give you that information without the consent of my Captain. With your resources, I would appreciate that you continue to find all you can; we need to find who is trying to steal the box. That's now the subject of our investigation."

The colors of the Pacific's horizon are changing as the sun begins to cast long shadows. The time has flown by and it is late afternoon, almost dinnertime. "We've taken a lot of your time, Malcolm, and I'm in your debt. Kathy and I are going up to Ventura for dinner and to spend the night in an old hotel we like there."

"Did you not want a tour of my collection?"

"Well yes I've been looking forward to seeing your cars and listening to the stories you have, but we've taken so much of your time now."

"You can make up for the time taken by ordering a large pepperoni pizza for us, then I will take you through a magical time of men and machines. As I mentioned earlier, all my records are stored in my computer, also all my pictures and illustrations. I have the chairs situated so that we can begin the tour by viewing some of the past events on the large screen TV. I have spare rooms for guests and it would be my pleasure to have you stay the night here."

"Kathy what do you think? We can go to Ventura anytime."

THE ARTIMUS BOX

"I think Malcolm's a most generous host. This whole day's been a lovely experience, and I would love to stay and absorb more of the early American racing history."

"I have some pictures that will aid in the feel of what it was like in the early days," Donner explains. "What you need to keep in mind is the lack of experience and knowledge the men building and driving the cars had.

"There were not any huge corporations with technical departments that were available to these innovators; the early engineering was done a great deal by instinct and the seat of the pants.

"The early gasoline was about sixty-octane in today's rating system. We have an 85 to 98 octane rating for our street vehicles now. This meant that the engine compression ratios were about five to one back then, as compared to the fourteen to one and higher compression ratios run today by some racing engines. The early brakes were on the rear wheels only and were cable operated. When the first hydraulic brakes came into use, they were primitive. They did not have rubber seals to retain the fluid; they used leather seals that were hand made by the racers.

"The brake fluid was anything that would not rust or freeze. Leaks and total failures were common.

"To understand the significance of the hydraulic system I would like to tell you a story about the 1921 French Grand Prix.

"Some powers in France made it known that they would welcome some American cars to come to the French Grand Prix and have them race against Europe's finest cars. The American Duesenberg team was the only team to take up the challenge. They were able to have Albert Champion of Champion Spark Plugs pay the entry fees and transportation costs of the cars to France. Champion, who had been born in France and was a rags-to-riches American success story, wanted to show off his new wealth.

"The cars arrived in France with Duesenberg's almost standard road car hydraulic braking system, which at the time did not attract much attention from the French. The advantage the system had was an equal amount of braking effort to each wheel, and an automatic adjustment for wear during the course of the event.

"The racecourse was laid out on public roads consisting of compacted sand and stone, during practice for the event there were many crashes due to the slippery surface.

"Jimmy Murphy, driving one of the four Duesenberg's, crashed due to the front brakes working too well and broke a rib. He removed some of the brake lining material from the front brakes so that the front brakes would not lock up, taped up his ribcage and went out to race. Jimmy and his Duesenberg just flew. He could brake much later getting into the turns and could do it all day long. No one could catch him. He averaged 78 miles per hour for the 321 miles of the race and finished 15 minutes ahead of the second-placed French Ballot car. One can only imagine the beating Murphy had to endure driving over the rough roads, and for over four hours.

"The French were outraged. They did not play The Star Spangled Banner, even though it was the custom of the day to play the anthem of the winner's country.

THE ARTIMUS BOX

Murphy got a small medal for winning the race and the team decided it was time to leave.

"Before they could go, the French seized Murphy's car because a French brake company wanted to protect what it claimed were its legal rights to the Duesenberg's brake system. However due to the ridiculous nature of the complaint the car was quickly released.

"Moreover, our hero, Albert Champion, was taken into custody by the gendarmes, and told that because he was born in France, and had not done his military service, he was under arrest as a deserter. It was all the American embassy could do to get him back to the United States. Champion never went back to France after that.

"The international press wrote that the Duesenberg cars were basically production cars and had beaten the best European racing cars of the time. The Duesenberg's, with American-made better brakes, Miller carburetors and Firestone tires, were the best of the day. Four-wheel hydraulic brakes had proven their worth in racing. The Duesenberg cars were the big luxury cars of the twenty's. The company went under, as did so many others in the great depression. The cars were the source of the term, 'That's a Duesy,' meaning something special, or nice.

"The engines of the day were another challenge.

"As I mentioned earlier, the fuel that was available in the early days was very low in octane rating, which meant that the engines would knock, vibrate, and ultimately blow up if you pressed them too hard. The knocking noise is actually the sonic waves colliding in the cylinder.

"This violent vibration will melt pistons, and hammer the connecting rods and bearings, and can lead to total destruction of the engine. The early pioneers knew you could not let the engines knock for long or the engine would destroy itself. The engines had small cylinder bores, long crankshaft strokes and low compression ratios to keep the knocking to a minimum.

Van gets up from his seat to stretch. Kathy asks if they would like her to make coffee. Both men readily agree. "Malcolm, I don't know if Kathy told you her grandfather was one of those early racers. She has his trophy collection. I never met the man but hearing you talk, those guys must have been super men."

"My impression of them is that they were very stout fellows indeed. I have interviews with some of the pioneers who drove the cars. One man told me that in the early nineteen hundreds a company gave him some alcohol to use as fuel. He could not make it work with the carburetors he had, and ended up using the alcohol for washing parts. It was much later that the fuel companies started to use additives to stop the knocking and bring up the octane rating. Before the fuel companies improved the gasoline, the racers were experimenting with different additives to gain horsepower. Each step made was by trial and error. Fires, explosions, lost lives were all a part of the learning process. Never the less our intrepid heroes kept at it. Most of these men raced for a living; racing put food on the table.

"Men like Leon Duray and Frank Lockhart are two of the early heroes that were instrumental in furthering engine development with fuels and supercharging.

THE ARTIMUS BOX

"Leon Duray experimented with methanol as a fuel, what we call a wood alcohol, and found that it gave much better power. You could use higher compression with no knocking. For the 1926 season, the rules committee reduced the engine capacity from 122 cubic inches to 91 cubic inches to reduce the speed of the cars for reasons of safety. They thought that too many lives had been lost due to the high speeds. In early 1926, 150 horsepower from 91 cubic inches was very good power. This was a supercharged engine using gasoline with a small amount of benzol and tetraethyl lead added.

"Duray, using his mix of fuels, started getting 200 horsepower, then 225, then 250, then 270. Remember, this was eighty years ago, and by an engine with less than 1500cc's or 91 cubic inches.

"Frank Lockhart is credited with going 171 miles an hour with the same type of 91 cubic inch engine, in a Miller racing car at Muroc Dry Lake in 1927. Some mathematicians equate this speed to have taken 285 horsepower to achieve. As you can see, the numbers are very impressive. The early men were fearless and the progress and engineering were phenomenal.

"The early pioneers tried everything to make the automobile better, front wheel drive, four wheel drive, rear wheel drive, and fully independent suspension on all four wheels. They tried front engine, rear engine, and mid-engine placements.

Even a monocoque racecar called a Cornelian pre-dated Colin Chapman's famous Lotus racing cars by a half a century."

Chapter 22

Malcolm Donner's phone has been ringing every few minutes for most of the time he and the Taylors have been visiting. Finally, Malcolm has had enough and goes to answer the phone and stop the annoying phoning.

Malcolm returns to the room and excitedly tells Van and Kathy that the phone call was from a man that was most insistent that Donner authenticate a book of Artimus drawings that he had purchased from an internet source. Donner is very animated and is thinking that the book of Artimus drawings described by the person phoning is very likely the book that was stolen from his house ten years ago. He asks Van to advise him what he should do to get the book back.

"Did you get his name or phone number Malcolm?"

"No, I told him to come right over and gave him my address. All I could think of was getting my book back."

"Okay. Call the police and have them stand by. Give them all the information you can and let them know that I am here. This is my badge number. Do you know how long it will take the person to get here?"

THE ARTIMUS BOX

"He said he would be here within an hour. I think he might have bought the book in good faith. He said he knew of my collection and would be willing to pay for my time."

"Malcolm, buying stolen property, even in good faith, does not give him any right to that property. As long as you can prove it belongs to you, the book will be returned to you."

"I have an insurance identification number stamped in the book and the papers to prove it."

Van looks to Kathy, "This may be a good lead in Artimus box case. Malcolm let's first see if it is your book and then find out what information we can get from the man. See if the police can send someone here before the man gets here. This is not in my jurisdiction but I can assist you in making a citizen's arrest if that becomes necessary."

Malcolm calls the police and describes the events to them. The police promise to send a uniformed man over in an unmarked car. When the uniformed police officer arrives, he is ushered to the dining room where he waits with Van and Kathy.

Thirty-five minutes later the doorbell of the Donner residence rings. Donner opens the front door to meet a tall thin man, dressed in dark brown corduroy pants and matching sport jacket. He has with him a large aluminum brief case. The man removes his brown felt snap-brim hat to reveal a balding head. He extends his hand to Donner and introduces himself as Doctor Scott Hall. Donner shakes the man's hand, and says that he is Malcolm Donner and is happy to meet him.

"Please come in Doctor Hall. I did not ask your name on the phone but I presume that you are the man with the Artimus drawings."

"Yes, you are quite right Mister Donner. I am very anxious to have you look at the book. I am thrilled to have it. I have been collecting Artimus items for two years now and just cannot believe my luck in being able to find this."

"Please come into my study and show me your book sir."

Hall goes to a table and sets his briefcase down. He opens the case and takes out the book.

"May I bring you something to drink Mr. Hall? I am going to make some tea. Would you like some?"

"Yes, please that would be very nice."

Donner goes to the dining room barely able to contain his excitement. He whispers, "That is my book; I knew it was my book as soon as he took it out of his brief case."

The police officer says, "I'll go in with you to question the man now. I would like you to show me your proof of ownership with the man present."

As the two men go into Donner's study, Doctor Hall looks quite startled and tries to put the book back into his brief case.

"Sir, please stand away from the briefcase," the officer says.

"What is this some kind of hold up?" cries Doctor Hall. "Mr. Donner please tell me what you mean by this; tell this man who I am."

"Sir, I am Officer Cleven with the Santa Monica police. I am here at Mr. Donner's request to investigate the theft of a book from him. Step away from the book now. I will not hesitate to handcuff you and take you into custody right now if you do not comply with my orders."

Doctor Hall looks around the room with wide eyes as if he is going to bolt. The police officer's hand goes to his pepper spray holster. All of the air seems to go out of the man and he steps away from the brief case with a loud sigh.

"Please show some identification sir. Do you have any weapons on your person?"

"No, no, officer I do not carry weapons. I am a Doctor of Science from the University of New Mexico. Here is my driver's license and university card."

"Thank you. Please have a seat. I need to determine ownership of the book and then you can tell your side of the story. Mister Donner, can you positively identify the book as your property?"

"Yes, officer I can. I have the insurance papers here and I can show you the identification number I put into the book."

"Okay, tell me the number and where I will find it in the book."

"The number is 1819GB75, and it will be on the inside of the book's front cover."

"Thank you Mister Donner." The officer opens the book and looks inside the front cover. He turns through a few pages in the book to verify its contents and inspects the rear cover. "Can I please see your insurance papers? Yes I see. This paper does conclusively identify this book as your property, Mister Donner."

"Mister Hall, I will return your driver's license and university card to you as soon as I run this through my department's I.D. section. Tell me how you come to have this stolen property sir."

"Officer, I have some of my students looking for Artimus artifacts as part of our class project. My subject for this term is twentieth century metal crafts. It involves the early use of manufactured materials for use as high strength, lightweight steel alloys used in racing and war materials. Yesterday, one of my students showed me an internet advertisement for this book. I emailed the address and asked for information about the book's origins and the price of the book.

"I received an answer with pictures of the book and a printed newspaper article. The article contained a story about an Artimus collector who died in a house fire about ten years ago. The person I corresponded with said that he was the son of the man in the article and that he found the book last year among some of the things he found on his father's property.

"He said he found it in a fireproof filing cabinet his father had in the house. I just took it for granted that the story in the paper was true and that the man was who he said he was. I took the first available flight to Los Angeles. I couldn't believe my luck." Doctor Hall sits down, his cheeks puff out as he blows out a long sigh. "I should have known better."

Officer Cleven calls into his department. He covers the mouthpiece with his hand. "Mister Hall, I'll need the name and address of the person you bought the book from. We need to apprehend this person as soon as possible."

"I met him at an internet café in Sherman Oaks, officer. He said he was moving to the east coast and that his house was a mess. He didn't want to meet there.

THE ARTIMUS BOX

He told me his name was Kim Derby junior. I've been very foolish. I should have asked for some identification. I was so happy to get the book before someone else got it that I just did not think. The man told me that I was the first person to answer his ad and that he had taken the ad off the internet as soon as we agreed on the price. I gave him a credit card number to use as a deposit on the book."

"Mister Donner, do you want to press charges against this man?"

"No, I do not officer. I just want to have my book back. I think it would be best to check out his identification. I am sure you will want to get a full statement from him."

Dr. Hall says, "Mister Donner, I am so sorry that the book was stolen from you, but now that you have it back, I am out $15,000.00 and I don't know any way to get it back."

The officer asks, "Do you have the emails that you sent, Mister Hall?"

"Yes I do, I saved them on my computer at the university."

"Officer, can we get your computer scam department to trace the email?" Donner asks.

"Yes, we can do that. I'll take Mister Hall with me to the department. I will need to take the book also as evidence. We may need to keep it for quite some time if we can get a lead on the person that sold it."

"Let me call your Chief before you take the book. He and I are old friends. I met him when he came to investigate the robbery here ten years ago. I hope I can keep the book until you might need it."

Van is waiting in the kitchen with Kathy; he did not want to hinder the Santa Monica officer. He opens the kitchen door to see want is going on, and after listening to the conversations between the men, he steps into the room with them.

"Mister Hall, my name is Van Taylor. I'm an investigator with the L.A.P.D. I think you may want to call your credit card company. I'd be willing to bet that the person calling himself Kim Derby will be adding charges to your card.

"We may be able to track him from where he uses the card. The credit card company can deny the charges. We can ask that whenever the card number is used again the location of the request be identified."

"I'll call the card people now, Mister Taylor. Thank you for the suggestion. Mister Donner, do you think I could come back later and look through the book with you? I've read all the books you've written on Harry Artimus. I know you're the foremost authority on all things Artimus. The main reason I sought your authentication was to be able to use the book as a qualified reference."

"I do let a select group of people use my library as a base of reference material. I am sorry someone tricked you, and that you may lose a great deal of money. Your loss, sir, is my fortunate gain, but I would be pleased to have you study the book at length here in my home."

Officer Cleven asks Doctor Hall to come with him to the police department. The police will have him go through the mug books, to try to identify the person that sold the book to him.

"Malcolm, I keep hearing ten years ago; the theft of the book from your house was ten years ago. Then a

THE ARTIMUS BOX

death of an Artimus collector, also ten years ago. Kathy tells me that Phil Manley was one of the most prominent men in the business of historic car restorations. His business began to decline, once again about ten years ago. Do you know of Kim Derby, Malcolm? Did he own the Artimus book of drawings at one time?"

"To answer your question about the book of drawings, I bought the book from Leo Deerman in 1965; Kim Derby never owned the book. As to Kimberly Derby, I did know him. He was in the film business in Hollywood in the seventies and eighties. He made a lot of money and many enemies.

"He was one of the Hollywood types that talked a good story, a real back-slapper, your best friend to your face and a knife in your back if he thought it would help him climb the ladder of success.

"He got into historic cars when the top Hollywood directors and producers were all into the scene. He bought the Artimus Malibu ranch and anything of Artimus importance he could get his hands on. He tried to buy my collection. First with a story that he was building a museum that would be a shrine to Harry Artimus.

"Then, when I refused, he became abusive and issued some threats. He said that he would contest my ownership of the Artimus artifacts. I have records and documentation of almost every piece I have ever collected. I registered everything with my insurance company, and all of the taxes are paid. This is not the case with many collectors; I think Derby thought he could bluff me into selling to him. He could be a very nasty character; I went out of my way not to be around him.

"He was found dead in the burned out remains of his house. The final reports that I read said that he was murdered and the house had deliberately been set on fire to try to hide the murder. I do not think his murderer has ever been found."

Chapter 23

"I hope that you will not change your plan to stay the night here. We can still have a great evening and I do want to show you my car collection tomorrow."

"Sounds good to me, Malcolm. I need to call my Captain and fill him in on the latest developments. We need to get a fix on the man who sold your book to Doctor Hall. The Captain will need to liaise with the Santa Monica P.D. We'll need access to Doctor Hall's computer email address to be able to track the emails he had with the man portraying Derby. Let me call in and we'll be able to plan from there."

"If you would like to phone from the living room, Kathy and I can go in the other room to watch some racing film footage I have from the Beverly Hills board track."

"Okay, thank you, I won't be long."

The living room of the home has a completely different feel to it from the study. This room has the feel of a woman's touch, the soft lemon yellow wall colors and the sun's setting rays coming through the gauze curtains highlight the highly polished end tables. Van sits on a lovely green leather couch and gazes at an oil painting of the rugged coastline. He picks up the phone receiver from the set on one of the end tables to call in.

"Captain, I've got some developments from Malcolm Donner's house. Kathy and I came to see what Donner had found on the Wahl murder and he's cleared up a lot for us. I'll write up a full report when I get back to the station."

Van brings the Captain up to date and asks what orders he has for him. The Captain says he will liaise with the Santa Monica P.D. and get the computer squad to work on finding the Derby perpetrator. He tells Van that if they need him he will call. "Stay in the city and take it easy."

After he finishes his call to the Captain, he goes into the room to watch the film footage Donner is showing Kathy. When the film ends, Van asks Donner to let him ask some questions.

"Malcolm I need to bring my notes up to date and I want to see what you know about Phil Manley. As I said before the ten-year thing keeps bugging me. Kathy mentioned to me that Manley's business has been going downhill, she says most of his customers and employees have left him. I take it that this was around the same time as the Derby murder. Did Manley know Derby?"

"Why yes, I think Phillip Manley and Kimberly Derby were quite friendly.

"Phil did most of the restoration work on the cars Derby had and Phil was very distressed about the Derby murder. Some people in the local restoration circle believe that Phil has become an alcoholic since the death of Derby.

THE ARTIMUS BOX

"Derby, at the time of his death, had sold most of his car collection. The cars he had remaining were in museums or at Manley's shop. The big movie men who had been into the historic car scene sold off their cars by that time and were off to the next fad. We all thought that Derby would sell off his collection and, when his cars went up for sale, we were sure that was the case.

"I was surprised that Derby kept his Artimus artifacts. I think that he had a genuine respect for them. I know that he kept the old Artimus ranch and was doing some archaeological work there."

"Would Manley have killed Derby for his collection, Malcolm? Did Derby have something in his Artimus stuff worth killing for, or did he and Manley have any money problems?"

"I do not have an answer to either question Van. I would hate to think Phil Manley capable of such a thing. It is true that shortly after Derby's death, Phil did become despondent and a few years after that his wife left him and took their children with her."

"Well that's enough detective work for the night Malcolm. Let's enjoy the rest of the evening. Kathy needs some time off from all of this and so do I. We're both looking forward to seeing your cars tomorrow."

Van, Kathy, and Donner enjoy an evening with great stories about racing and Van's tales of cops and robbers. Kathy recounts her own racing stories and some of the funny things that happen in her embroidery business. It is past midnight before Donner shows them to their room for the night.

When the Taylors awaken, the sun is just peeking through their bedroom window. The morning is fresh and clean. From the Donner home, they can smell the ocean air. Van is up and off to shower and shave.

Kathy fluffing her pillow says, "Don't use up all the hot water please. I need to wash my hair."

Van finishes his shower and tells Kathy that he is going to the kitchen to see about some coffee.

As Van walks down the hall towards the kitchen, he can smell the rich aroma of coffee brewing. He also hears voices; one voice is that of Malcolm Donner. The other voice is feminine and asking Donner about their weekend plans.

As Van enters the kitchen, Donner and the woman have their backs to him, the woman is cooking on the stove, and Malcolm has his arm around her waist, with his chin resting on her shoulder.

Van takes a couple of steps back and starts whistling before he reenters the kitchen again.

"Good morning Malcolm, do I smell coffee?"

"Oh good morning Van. I would like you to meet, um, my housekeeper Mrs. Lansing."

Mrs. Lansing is a tall slender woman. She has short brown hair, and glasses that are attached to a fine silver chain around her neck. Van thinks she is probably in her fifty's; she smiles readily and seems a warm, kindly woman.

"Mrs. Lansing, this is Van Taylor. He is Kathy Taylor's husband and will be having breakfast with us this morning."

"It is so nice to meet you Mister Taylor. Mister Donner has been telling me all about your adventures."

"Please call me Van, Mrs. Lansing. We have had a wonderful evening. Kathy and I are looking forward to seeing Malcolm's car collection today."

THE ARTIMUS BOX

"How do you take your coffee, Van?"

"Just black please."

"Mrs. Lansing is making a wonderful breakfast for us; her very special French toast. She bakes the bread herself and let me tell you, it is delightful."

"That sounds wonderful. Kathy's in the shower and will join us in a couple of minutes. Have you been with Malcolm long Mrs. Lansing?"

"Yes, I lost my husband to cancer ten years ago and Malcolm has been very kind and supportive of me over the years."

"I was just telling Mrs. Lansing about the gentleman last night, Van. She was the lady that found the men robbing me of the book ten years ago. She was very smart to have realized what was happening so quickly and getting clear of the house before they could do her any harm. She called the police and helped them in the robbery investigation. I was away on a business matter and Mrs. Lansing called me to inform me of the break in, and theft. She is still very careful about entering the house when I am away."

Kathy enters the kitchen, her hair still damp. "My, it smells just wonderful in here," Kathy exclaims.

Malcolm Donner initiates the introductions. "Kathy this is Mrs. Lansing; Mrs. Lansing this is Van's wife Kathy Taylor."

"I am pleased to meet you Mrs. Lansing. This kitchen is fantastic and I smell French toast. I didn't think I could be hungry after all the food we ate yesterday."

Donner says, "We can go to the dining room and let Mrs. Lansing finish her cooking. She will be joining us for breakfast."

Mrs. Lansing brings the breakfast into the dining room with help from Kathy. The platters are stacked with the French toast, scrambled eggs, and fresh fruits. They eat breakfast with enthusiasm and Van and Kathy compliment Mrs. Lansing on her cooking. Malcolm pushes back from the table saying he is ready to conduct the tour of his car collection. Kathy wants to help with the dishes and tells Van she will meet them when she is finished.

The men help to bring the dishes into the kitchen and, after putting the dishes on a counter, Donner turns to Van and says, "Let's get to the garage before the women put us to work."

Donner leads the way to the entrance of the garage from the kitchen. As they step through the door, Donner snaps on the lights. The garage is one long room; all of the garages that at one time stood individually attached to the bungalows now join with some clever support beams and archways.

The joining gives the impression of a much larger space. There is some small metal working machinery and an array of tools. The room is clean and bright, each car has a workbench dividing it from the next car. The floor, painted a light grey color, adds to the clean look of the room. There are a number of engines displayed in glass cases and metal shelves with cylinder heads and gleaming engine parts.

"Malcolm, do you do all of your own restorations?"

"I try to do as much as I can Van, but some of the engine and transmission work is a bit too much for me. I send the major engine and transmission work to a man

THE ARTIMUS BOX

in Sonoma. He is my secret. The man is meticulous and does first rate work."

"Sonoma, I'll be. Small world Malcolm, we have some friends there. For such a small town it's a treasure. The town has great restaurants, and a gorgeous countryside, and my all time favorite red wine."

"I agree completely, I do enjoy going for the vintage races there and I usually stay over a few days just to relax and drive around."

They continue to walk into the far end of the garage space.

There are five cars in the space and Van finds the size of an old four-place touring car amazing. It takes up a lot of the space. The behemoth dwarfs the other cars of this beautiful collection.

"What kind of car is this Malcolm?"

"It is a 1911 Lozier. Van, this is one of the first well-built and designed American cars. The car was the Cadillac of the day; the Europeans did not rate America as an automobile maker in those days. Most of our cars were rudely constructed and not very reliable. Parts were not interchangeable and reliability and performance were poor. Lozier changed all of that; a first rate car.

"Harry Lozier was one of the men that got into the bicycle business towards the end of the 1800's. He made beautiful bicycles that were very well made and far ahead of his competition. He made sewing machines that were also premier machines. His business was so much better than his competitors that, in 1897, he sold the business for four million dollars cash.

"This car is one that Harry Artimus bought after he had sold one of his carburetor businesses to a group from New York; the car cost $7800.00 in 1911. That was many times more than any other cars of the time. Harry Artimus was a man that made and lost a lot of money in his time."

Van stands by the car looking up at the steering wheel. "The car is just so huge, I look at this car and then the car in the next space over and the difference in the sizes is incredible."

Malcolm walks to the next car. "As you can see, the rate of progress was substantial. We also had a world war in the years between these two cars.

"The war brought a lot of change, much better engineering, and a big increase in power outputs. The next car marks the beginning of the Artimus cars' stranglehold on Indianapolis race wins. It has much more horsepower than the Lozier does and as you have pointed out, it is much smaller and lighter weight. With the increase in power, these cars were faster and a lot more agile than the earlier cars."

At this point Kathy comes into the garage from the kitchen.

"I wanted to help Mrs. Lansing with the dishes and cleaning up after breakfast, but she's sent me to the boys in the garage with orders to enjoy your collection, Malcolm."

"I am pleased that Mrs. Lansing sent you Kathy. I am showing the Lozier that was Harry Artimus' first personal luxury road-car. Would you like me to start over?"

"No please go ahead. I've actually read about the Lozier cars and some of the races that Ralph Mulford won with the cars."

THE ARTIMUS BOX

"You are quite correct Kathy; I am impressed. We were just discussing the difference in the size of the cars; the next car is an example of the progress made in the twelve years between the Lozier and the Artimus 122 car. The Artimus car is 24 inches wide and 32 inches tall and weighs in at 1400 pounds. This is the 122 cubic inch engine car, a beautiful example of a pure racing machine. The contest board thought these cars were too fast for the time. The sanctioning body decided to limit the next cars to 91 cubic inches in order to slow them down. By setting this car beside the Lozier, you are struck by the difference in size.

"The next car is the 91 cubic inch car; you can see the refinements Artimus made from the 122 cars. The 91's were Harry's jewels; he brought supercharging to an art and blew everyone away. This car is one of those jewels. Let me take the hood off and show you the engine."

Malcolm removes the hood and lays it on the adjacent workbench. The engine gleams in the lights of the garage. The polish of the aluminum cam covers and the nickel plating of the water pipes flaunt how delicately sculptured the entire engine is. They add to the clean overall beauty of the machinery.

"Man, oh man. Were the cars this clean and polished in those days?" Van asks. "I have seen some restorations where the people polish and chrome plate everything."

"No this is the way the cars left Harry's plant. This is a very true to the original car and, as you can see, Harry was a perfectionist. This car with Harry's supercharger genius was much faster than the 122 cubic inch cars and the 91's won most of the races of the day."

"Wow!" exclaims Van. "It's just amazing to see how beautiful and well designed this car is. I can really see what passion is in these cars and what passion and pride you must have in owning this car."

"These cars do bring me great pleasure, and I am so fortunate that the people who robbed me did not take the cars. I have invested a good deal of money in rebuilding the doors to the garage while keeping the appearance of the original carriage house doors. In order to keep any ultra violet rays from bleaching any of the surfaces, there is no direct sunlight. I had the indirect lighting installed to keep the interior bright and had the alarm and fire systems installed to hopefully avoid any further break-ins.

"I would like to direct your attention to this next car. This is the car, or I should say most parts of this car were the basis for the Kline car. You can see how much larger this car is than the 91 cubic inch car. This is the V-16 four-wheel drive car. The same car that Harry wanted to destroy after his dealings with Horst Kline. Fred Offlower saved this car from Harry's wrath, and they sold the car right before the Indianapolis race that year, but the car did not perform that well.

"With the depression of the economy in the early 1930's, the rules board wanted to bring in race cars that would not be as expensive as the Artimus cars that sold for $15,000.00. Harry, because of the change in the rules, had to remove the supercharger to be able to compete at Indianapolis that year. I believe he did not have enough time to develop the camshafts and carburetion to make this engine, in normally aspirated form, produce enough horsepower to be competitive. The rules also stated that the cars had to have a riding mechanic, reverting to the early days, which is why the car is so much larger.

"The rules makers were convinced that the public wanted to see two people in each car. However, this was very dangerous for the person riding beside the driver. This was well before any thoughts of seat belts.

"You can imagine what a hard crash would do to a person riding alongside the driver and trying to hang on to anything he could grab. It was not until the 1960's that the auto racing rules makers demanded the use of seat belts in racing cars. Many drivers felt that they would have a better chance of survival if they could get clear of a crashing car, or even jumping out of a racecar at high speed. An American driver, racing in Europe in the 1950's, was famous for jumping out of race cars that were on fire or were, he thought, about to crash."

Van's eyes are dancing from one exhibit to the next. "I see that you collect other items that you have on the shelves. Are they all from the Artimus cars?"

"Well yes, the shelves have a 91 cubic inch engine that is a piece of artwork. I had the man in Sonoma build it up from parts I collected. He did an outstanding job on it, and I love looking at it as art. The other pieces are from the Artimus cars and engines. Some of the parts are ones that failed during a race and, even they have artistry.

"My late wife collected the sewing machines over by the last stall. One is a very early Lozier and the one next to it is a White. Both of those companies went on to build early American automobiles."

Kathy asks, "What kind of car is in the next stall Malcolm? It looks much smaller than all of the other cars."

"This is a quarter midget car. This was my first racecar. My father bought this car for me to race when I was 8 years old. I have some great memories from racing all over Southern California with my father.

"We met many people who have become the best friends I have had in my life. It was low cost fun that brought me to my love of racing and the fine art of machinery."

"How long did you race, Malcolm?"

"I raced this car until my Father died. I was 12 then and that was the upper age limit with that club."

"It is so tiny, Malcolm, but I can picture you racing the car. Did you win with it?"

"I did win some races after the first two years; it took me that long to learn the right way to race and how to get by the other cars without wrecking. I was not the fastest boy out there, but it did teach me sportsmanship and I became much closer to my father. He loved to help me work on the car.

"He and my mother and I would go to a fairground where our club held the races. We would have picnics with the food my mother made. We had a lot of fun together as a family.

"I have to say that racing made me a better person. It gave me purpose and focus. I knew that I had to do well in school, or my father would not let me race. I did not need to be with a street gang, or be with any criminal element, I had the excitement of racing and a cadre of good friends and good people, which I still care for to this day.

THE ARTIMUS BOX

"I apologize for going on like that, but racing is such a passionate sport. If more people had a passion and respect for what they do in life, I believe the world would be a better place."

The space that Donner has created by combining the four original garages is a delightful setting to display his car collection. It is like stepping back in time. The carriage house doors and the wood paneled interior add to the feeling. As they take time to drink in the ambiance of the space, Kathy looks up at the bright blue eyes of the man she loves. He is really enjoying the moment. Van smiles down at Kathy and says, "I know kid, it's time to go."

"Malcolm, this has been a wonderful visit for us. We really appreciate your hospitality. I can't tell you how much we've enjoyed you sharing your collection with us and the wonderful stories and insights you've given us. We're going to have to get going and prepare for tomorrow. I want to follow up on Phil Manley myself and I want to see where the investigation is going with our friend Doctor Scott Hall.

"I'll talk to the robbery division of the Santa Monica police and see where they are. We need to find the guy who sold your book. If we can locate the seller, we may be able to get a fix on who broke into your house. I'm thinking that the Derby murder may also be connected. All of this leads us back to the Artimus box. I need to connect the dots, and my brain has already gone numb trying to figure this puzzle out."

Donner shakes Van's hand. "I enjoyed having you two as guests and I hope we see more of each other. I would appreciate it if you could keep me abreast of the case. I will keep looking for information from my sources, and if I find anything I will let you know."

"I'd appreciate any information you can find, Malcolm, but please keep in mind that we've had murders. The people we're dealing with are dangerous. Please don't take any chances, okay? You know we'd really like to repay your hospitality; the next dinner is on us at our house.

"We'd like to say goodbye to Mrs. Lansing. Please bring her with you to visit us at our house in the Palisades. I inherited a grand old house from my parents. It's a small house like most of them that were built by the Reverend Charles H. Scott's religious commune sect. The house, being small, is offset by the large lot it's on and the fabulous views we have. I think you'd enjoy the craftsmanship that went into the house. It was built in 1924."

Kathy and Van say goodbye to Mrs. Lansing and are walking out to their car when Kathy asks Van about his invitation to Malcolm for dinner at their house.

"What was that all about with the Mrs. Lansing deal?"

"I didn't get a chance to tell you that when I went for coffee this morning I walked into the kitchen and found Malcolm with his arm around Mrs. Lansing's waist and his head was resting on her shoulder. She was asking him if they were still going to have time to be together today. I had to backtrack and make some noise before reentering the kitchen. I didn't want to embarrass them, or me, for that matter."

"I'm glad he has someone to be with, Van. They are both such nice people, they should be together."

THE ARTIMUS BOX

Chapter 24

Van is up with the sun on Monday morning. He is rested and ready to tackle his investigation of Phil Manley. Having cleared up the Tim Wahl murder to his satisfaction, Van wants to see if there is a connection between the Kim Derby murder and Phil Manley. Van knows that there are people that want the Artimus box, and whoever those people are, they must know about the diamonds. The diamonds are what make the box worth the trouble. The unknown persons have committed some serious criminal offenses to try to seize control of the box. Therefore, Van theorizes, someone has information about the box and diamonds that even Malcolm Donner is unaware of at this time.

Van has been on the internet looking for other prominent Artimus collectors, and with the information he has been able to find Donner and Kim Derby were the two men who possessed the bulk of artifacts.

Van reasons that although there are other possibilities, the most probable is that Derby had the most complete information about the box. He believes Derby's murder was for that information.

Van knows that old cold cases are the most difficult to solve and the most time consuming, but in order to solve this case, he feels he must find the origin, to find what put all of this in motion. Phil Manley is the next logical step.

It is just coming up on 6:30 when Van decides to make hotcakes and eggs for breakfast; he hears Kathy go into the shower. He finds the hotcake mix that only requires him to add water. The last time he tried to make hotcakes from flour, they were a disaster. He cooks the eggs over easy and adds them between the hotcakes. The buttered hotcakes are without syrup. After a good breakfast, they can both go off to work ready for whatever the day will bring. Kathy comes into the kitchen with her usual bright enthusiasm. She is rarely out of sorts and her light mood and engaging personality is a reason she has always been popular.

Kathy is delighted by Van making a good breakfast; the usual start of the day is a hurried cup of coffee, a quick kiss and then off to work.

Van gets back to work, finding Manley is an altogether different problem. He phones Manley's shop in Long Beach several times but no one answers the phone. There is an answering machine with a message from Manley to leave a number and he will call back. Van checks with DMV records to find Manley's home address. After obtaining the address and phone number, he tries the home phone to no avail. The next step is to find any cell phone numbers Manley might have. Van goes through various cell phone company records looking for a number for Manley. After an hour of calls to the companies, and identifying himself as a police officer with a special code, he finds a cell number registered to Manley. He dials the number and lets the phone ring. After quite a number of rings, a subdued Manley answers.

"Hello, hello, who is this?"

"Phil, this is Van Taylor. I've been trying to contact you. I'd like to talk to you about the Artimus box."

"Oh, uh, hi. I'm just getting up."

"Are you at home, Phil? I've been calling your home number."

"Uh, no, I, uh, am staying with a, uh, friend. I'm, not at home. Look, I'm a little groggy. Can I call you back?"

"Phil, I need to see you today. I can meet you at your shop in an hour."

"Uh, give me a couple of hours and I can meet you at the shop. I was going to sleep in today, but I would like to know what you have found in the box."

"I'll see you there. Let me give you my mobile number in case you're going to be late."

Van heard Manley say, 'In the box.' He caught that and wonders if that means he knows about the diamonds, and, if so, how does he know? That and what else does he know?

Van checks out an unmarked car from the police garage and takes his small digital camera that can record sound as well as pictures and is so small he can carry it in a shirt pocket. The trip down the San Diego freeway in late morning traffic is not bad. Van gets to Manley's shop to find the place closed. There are no lights on and no sign of anyone inside. He walks around the building to see if there is another door in the back. As he goes around the corner of the building, he hears a loud motorcycle coming into the parking lot.

As Van turns back and walks toward the front of the building, he sees a man riding a motorcycle around his car.

The man turns and rides to the front of Manley's shop and throws something through one of the windows. As Van comes around the corner, the man on the motorcycle sees him and turns toward him. The man riding the motorcycle accelerates it hard; the bike is coming at him fast. Ten yards from Van the motorcycle abruptly stops and by spinning the rear wheel of the bike the rider pivots around and roars out of the parking lot. Van rubs his eyes. The dust and gravel thrown up by the spinning rear tire of the fleeing motorcycle temporarily blind him.

He cannot see well enough through the dust to get a license number. The man riding the motorcycle is huge. He wonders if he surprised the man or if the man recognized him.

Phil Manley arrives some time later and gets out of his car. Manley's disheveled appearance is quite a change since Van last saw him. Manley is unshaven and looks shrunken, his cheeks are hollow and his face is ashen. He walks as if he is bearing the weight of the world on his shoulders.

Van speculates that Manley does have the look of an alcoholic in the advanced stages of the disease. Manley shuffles his feet instead of walking. He unlocks the front door of his shop and does not seem to notice Van or the broken front window. Van calls out, and Manley is startled and turns quickly to close the door in Van's face.

"Phil, it's Van Taylor. We have an appointment," he shouts.

THE ARTIMUS BOX

Manley is shuffling as quickly as he can to the back of his shop. He stops and very slowly turns to see Van at the door. His whole body seems to relax and he returns to the front door to open it for Van to enter.

Van comes through the front door and says to Manley, "Phil, are you alright?"

"Uh I just haven't been sleeping well. Business hasn't been so good lately and I guess I'm just worn a little thin by it."

"Why don't we go get some lunch Phil? I know I'm hungry and some coffee would taste good too."

"No I don't want to go out. I'm not really hungry. I can make us some coffee here if you'd like."

"Yes I'd like some coffee if you don't mind. The reason I wanted to see you today is to ask some questions about Kim Derby. I understand that you were a good friend to Derby. Is that correct Phil?"

"Uh, yes, Kim and I were friends. I did many of his restorations. At one time Kim owned five excellent examples of Harry Artimus' finest cars and I did all of the work on the cars. What does Kim have to do with the Artimus box?" Manley recognizes his mistake, his eyes dart away from Van.

Van sees the look and asks, "Why did you think of Derby in connection to the Artimus box?"

"Well isn't that the reason you said you wanted to see me? You said you had questions about the box right?"

"Yes you're absolutely right, Phil. I just didn't know until now that there was a connection between the two. I'm glad to have that cleared up. Now you can tell me what the connection was, and how you would know about the contents of the box."

Manley sits up in his chair and looks angry. "What do you mean I cleared it up for you? Are you trying to trick me?"

"I'm not trying to trick you. I have persons unknown that are trying to get the Artimus box by any means. I have an unsolved murder of Kim Derby. I have a break-in and theft of Artimus stuff from Malcolm Donner, and guess what the common denominator is Phil? Right now buddy, that's you. You've known the injured parties. I'm not here to trick you. I'm here to find some answers to these crimes.

"I can tell you that a new development in the case has just opened. A book of drawings by Leo Deerman that was stolen from Donner's home ten years ago, has just turned up.

"A person who claims to be the son of Kim Derby sold the book to a man we have as a witness. I've checked the marriage and birth records for Kim Derby and his wives, and I do not find a son born to his wives of record. Do you know of a son to Derby? Is there something I'm missing here Phil? I need some help here man, I thought you'd be the first one to want to help me get to the bottom of all this. Kim Derby was a good friend of yours, wasn't he, Phil?"

Manley looks ill, his pallor has a grayish tint. "Uh this is a lot to take in, let me make you some coffee, and I need a drink."

Van knows Manley is stalling to get a story together, and he can see that Manley is deeply involved in this whole affair.

He thinks the best tack is to let Manley get a story together and for him to take it apart. Manley looks shaken and Van thinks that he is very close to breaking

THE ARTIMUS BOX

down. With a little more pressure, he thinks Manley will tell him the truth of his involvement.

Manley returns to the office with two coffee cups. He gives one to Van, and sits down behind his desk and takes a long drink from his cup. The color returns to Manley's face and his demeanor changes.

"What were you asking me, something about Kim Derby wasn't it?"

Van sees the change in Manley. The cup he is drinking from must have liquor in it Van thinks, this is probably his first drink of the day.

"I want to know if you have any information about Kim Derby's family. I'd also like to know what Derby's Artimus collection consisted of."

"You've asked too many questions for me to remember, but I did hear you say that the Deerman book of drawings was recovered. What does that have to do with Derby?"

"I don't think you heard me correctly Phil. The book was sold on the internet to a man by a person claiming to be Kim Derby's son."

"Look man you're the cop. I just don't see what any of that has to do with me. I don't want to be quizzed on this stuff. I've got problems of my own. I don't need yours too."

Manley is getting wound up. He does not seem to be able to stay with a thought, and Van is sure he has lost the chance to have him break down and confess all. He will not let Manley have that first drink when he questions him again.

"Phil, your friend was murdered and his Artimus collection was not in his house when it was deliberately set on fire. I wanted to give you a chance to help in bringing his killer to justice. Can you tell me what Derby had in his house at the time of his murder?"

"You don't get it. I'm tired and I have other troubles. I just don't want to talk any more. Leave me alone."

"Phil I'm sorry you feel that way, but I need answers. If you refuse to help me I'll bring you to the station house and formally interrogate you."

"You've got no right to threaten me. I get enough of that from, well, I mean, oh I don't know what I mean."

"Phil are you in trouble? Is someone threatening you? I can help you, Phil, if you will help me. Who is the guy on the motorcycle that threw something through your front window? Is that a threat to you Phil? Let's go look for whatever the guy threw and see if there is a note on it. I can help you. The department can protect you."

"No, no, no, leave me alone. I don't want your help. Just leave me alone. I don't want you mixing in my business. If you want to talk to me again you can talk to my attorney. Now leave, just get out."

Van looks at Manley. He has shrunken down in his chair; there is no doubt in his mind that Manley is deeply disturbed. As he walks out of the office, he hears Manley sob. Van walks through the shop looking for the object that the man on the motorcycle threw through the window. He follows a trail of broken glass and sees a short piece of steel pipe. The pipe is about one inch in diameter and four inches long, it has threads on each end. At first Van thinks, it could be a small bomb, but there are no caps on the ends of the pipe and there would be if the pipe were to explode. He cautiously

THE ARTIMUS BOX

picks up the pipe with his handkerchief and holds it at arms length. He looks in one end of the pipe.

There is a paper rolled up in the pipe. Van takes a small pair of tweezers from his knife and carefully pulls the paper out of the pipe. There is a note written on the paper. He spreads the note out on top of a workbench with his knife and small file he found on the bench. The scrawled note reads, "I can't find you at home or shop. I need names. Don't make me keep looking for you."

Manley comes out of his office with a bottle of scotch in one hand. He sees Van and yells, "What the hell are you doing, what have you got in your hand? I told you I want you to leave."

"I found a note in this pipe that the motorcycle rider threw. The note says he wants names. What does that mean Phil?"

Manley puts the bottle down on a bench and moves toward Van with a surprising newfound speed. He snatches the note off the workbench and starts to rip it to pieces.

Van tries to grab the note; Manley stumbles away from him and falls on his back, pieces of the note floating to the floor. Manley sits up with tears welling up in his eyes, he shakes with sobs and puts his hands to his face and breaks out in tears. Van is dismayed and concerned for Manley, and he tries to help him up.

"Get the hell away from me. I told you to leave. You bully me and then shove me on the ground. Are you going to beat me up to get your questions answered? I'm calling my lawyer, and the Long Beach police. Now get out."

Van backs away. "I didn't push you Phil. You stumbled and fell on your own, and you're not in the best of shape. The police will take note of that. It's obvious that you are under a lot of stress. I'd like to help you. I'm going to leave my card on your bench. You can tell your attorney you will be brought in for questioning."

Van leaves his card on the bench and puts his handkerchief with the pipe still in it in his pocket, and walks out of the shop.

Chapter 25

When Van returns to the police station, he finds a stack of messages on his desk. One of the messages is from the computer fraud department. They have located the computer used in the sale of the stolen Deerman-Donner book. The computer fraud section is located in the main LAPD Parker Center building. The huge new LAPD facility is still a year or two away from being finished.

He calls the number that Parker Center left on the message. Helen Ames who answers the phone sounds like a very young girl. Not what Van expected. He fights the urge to ask her age.

"I thought the Santa Monica PD had this case, Ms Ames."

"Yes they do, but I have a friend in the Santa Monica PD, and he bumped it up to Parker Center. He called me to help him find this computer because the person that is using it is trying to hide his location and is pretty clever about it. But I have found that he always uses the same computer at an internet café in Van Nuys to make his sales."

"Does that mean he is still using the same location now Ms. Ames?"

"Yes sir he is selling motorcycle parts right now but he seems to sell all sorts of stuff."

"Can you email him and try to keep him there until I can get to his location."

"How long will it take you to get there sir?"

"I'm leaving now. I should be there in an hour."

"Yes okay, I think I can keep him on the hook. I'll tell him that I want to buy something from him and that I will email him with a credit card number in an hour."

"Okay, great work Ms Ames. Now how will I know the person?"

"The computer he uses is one of eight that are installed at the café. I've found out that they are numbered by station. His is station number six. Call me when you're in position at the café and I'll make sure the perp is on that computer for you."

Van jumps into his unmarked police car and heads north on the San Diego freeway and over the hill into the San Fernando Valley. Going up Van Nuys Boulevard, he comes to the address and pulls into the café's parking lot. Van calls Ames on his cell at the entrance to the café.

"Ms Ames, Van Taylor here. I'm at the front door of the café. Is our man still here?"

"Yes sir, he is on station six. I'm sending him a phony card number now. I'll give you a moment to get into place and then send him a "you're busted" notice."

She hangs up before Van can tell her not to warn the man before he can place him under arrest. Van has not looked to see what avenues of escape the building has nor has he called for backup. As he looks for something that will tell which of the computers is at station six, he sees a big man stand up abruptly and knock over the chair he was sitting on. The man then runs toward the back of the building. Van runs after the man. As he passes the overturned chair behind a computer station, he sees a number six decal on the small niche.

Van hates chases but in this instance, he has no other choice. He sees the man at a door at the rear of the building. The man he is chasing is in his forties; he has very thin blonde hair and is grossly over weight. Van puts his badge on his shirtfront and yells to the man to stop. The man turns to see Van then bolts out of the door.

Van is trying to run by the people who are in the aisle playing video games. By the time he gets to the door, the man is nowhere in sight. Van runs to the alleyway and spots the man turning the corner. He runs to the corner and turns to follow the man. The man is running for the parking lot, his flabby upper body jounces as he runs. Van does not want to let him get to his car and get away. Van gains quickly on the fat man, but as he chases the man down, a car backs out, clips his right leg and sends him spinning to the ground. Van springs up immediately and runs after the fat man, who is getting into an old Volkswagen convertible.

The fat man backs out of the parking space and turns toward the lot exit. Van holds up his badge and yells for the man to stop. The fat man at first slows, and then speeds up. As he passes, Van grabs the door handle. The car bounds out of the parking lot and onto Van Nuys Boulevard with Van now grimly holding on to the door handle and wondering to himself just what he was going to do now. The fat man's car is gaining speed and Van is yelling at the man to stop.

Van sees a stop light ahead with cars blocking the road waiting for the signal light to change. The man slows and then turns across the oncoming traffic lanes and into a side street. Van is bouncing around and his shoes are dragging the street. He gets his knee up on the sideboard of the old car and then gets his other foot up on the sideboard. He pulls himself up to the door and yells for the man to stop. The man turns to see Van yelling right in his face. As the fat man turns to face him, the car turns left also and starts down an alleyway. Van has stopped being afraid and is now getting mad.

He yells for the man to stop one more time, and then grabs the steering wheel and pushes it hard right. The car crashes into some small trashcans and then a big dumpster and grinds to a stop. Sparks fly from the trash bin scraping along the brick wall.

In desperation, the fat man tries to push Van aside to get out of the car. Van has had enough. He punches the fat man hard in the face. The man screams and falls back into the car, his nose bleeding profusely.

Van pulls on the car's door handle. The hinges of the door screech in protest but after yanking on the door, it slowly yields.

He pulls the fat man out of the car. The man has blood all over the front of his shirt; his hands are covering his face. Van turns the man around, bends him over the car door, and rips his shirttail off. Then he turns the man around and puts the ripped shirt in his hands.

"Put this over your nose and lean your head forward until the bleeding stops." The man just looks uncomprehendingly at Van. Van takes the piece of shirt, folds it up and holds it to the man's nose. He then takes the man's elbow and pushes the hand against his still bleeding nose. Van does not want the fat man's blood on him.

A police car comes into the alley and pulls up behind the wrecked VW. Van takes his badge from his shirt pocket and holds it up in his hands. After identifying himself to the officers, they ask him what has happened, and Van goes through the story for them. One of the officers asks him if he needs to go to the hospital. Van first thinks the officer means the man whose nose is still bleeding.

"No sir," the officer says, "look at your knees sir."

Van's jeans are in tatters; his knees are bleeding and blood is all over his socks and shoes.

"This jerk tries to run me over, drags me down Van Nuys Boulevard on my knees and won't stop. If I could have gotten to my gun, I would have shot him. I'm lucky my toes aren't coming out of my shoes. Damn, a good pair of jeans and a new pair of high buck sneakers shot."

"Do you want him arrested, sir?" the officer asks.

"You bet I do, but I would like to do that myself and take him back to my department for processing. Can you guys take care of the vehicle and canvassing the internet cafe? We also need to get statements from anyone on the street that saw me getting dragged down the street by this clown. I can have my Captain call yours and smooth over any jurisdictional stuff."

"I don't see a problem sir. If you can give me the run down, I can write it up and have the paper work done."

"That sounds good to me. Thanks for the help guys."

The other officer has handcuffed one of the VW driver's hands behind his back to a belt loop on his pants, leaving one hand free to hold the rag to his nose. The officer removes the man's wallet in order to identify him; and he hands the wallet to Van.

"His California drivers license ID's him as Thomas Brock of Reseda. Should I call the paramedics for him?"

"Yeah, let's sit him down on the ground by his car and have him lean his head forward."

"Inspector if you'll give me the key to your car I'll go back up the street and bring it here for you."

Van looks at the officer's name above his badge." Thanks Officer Phaver. Well my friend, that is above and beyond the call of duty, but I really appreciate it. Here's the key. The car is an unmarked Crown Vic with state tags. Now let me see to our pal Tommy boy here. I can hardly wait to get him back to my precinct. I've a lovely time planned for him. I need to read him his rights."

Officer Phaver brings Van's car to the head of the alley.

The medical team arrives a short time later.

"Tommy, I'm going to take the handcuffs off so the Med Techs can take care of you."

One of the Techs swabs Brock's nose and checks him over for any other injuries or problems. The other tech takes Van into the medical van and has him take off his jeans. He cleans up the abrasions and picks out some small pebbles imbedded in Van's knees. After applying antiseptics, Van pulls his jeans back on and steps out of the med van. Van says to the med tech,

THE ARTIMUS BOX

"When you finish cleaning him up I need you to sign him off so I can process him. You can sign me off too.

"Tommy I'm going to put the handcuffs back on you and take you to my precinct where you will be formally charged with attempted murder of a police officer, resisting arrest, plus any other charges the D.A. will have. The next charges will be for the sale of stolen goods, fraud and grand theft. We should be able to put you away for the rest of your life."

"I've got nothing to say to you pigs."

These are the first words Tommy has said. The policemen look at each other and shake their heads.

Van says, "Well this is just how we like them, uncooperative and stupid. Can you men give me a hand getting bright boy into the car?"

The three men lift Brock up and Van puts the handcuffs back on him.

They make sure he can breathe and then put him in the back seat of Van's car. Officer Phaver offers to take some pictures of his injuries and Brock's for the arrest report. Van, with his knees skinned up and bloody, looks at the jeans he is wearing; they took most of the punishment. His shoes that had rubber soles that wrapped up the toe of the shoes flap loosely. The street's abrasion wore the soles' edges away.

On the drive to the precinct, Van tries to get Thomas Brock to talk. Brock will not answer any questions. He will only say that he will not answer any questions and remains stoic. Van parks in the back of the precinct and helps Brock out of the car.

He brings Brock to the booking desk. The sergeant asks Van what the charges are. Van lists the charges and tells the officer to take Brock to a holding cell.

"What do you think you're doing pig? You can't hold me like that, I got rights, man."

"For now, until I decide how helpful you want to be, I have a special plan for you and some inmates I want you to meet. I hope you won't talk until I can get you into a cell with Big Al and his friends."

"No man, I can't do that. I don't want to be in a cell with other guys. I'm not queer, man."

"Hey fat man, Big Al likes his fun. You look kind of soft to me, and Big Al likes his girls soft."

Van goes to his locker and changes his pants and socks. His shoes are ruined and he puts on his polished dress uniform shoes. He goes up the stairs to his desk, and runs a criminal history trace on Thomas Brock.

Van finds that Brock is a petty offender, with two DUI's. The only jail time he has done was for the DUI's. Brock does not strike Van as being a tough guy.

He thinks he's scared, but Van does not yet know just what he is scared of. So, for a while, Van is going to let Brock stew in a holding cell, and then he is going to try a different kind of scare to get him to talk.

Van told Brock he could hold him for 24 hours before he has to charge him or let him free. This is not true but he is going to run his bluff on Brock. He has enough charges to send Brock away, but he wants to know how Tommy got the Deerman/Donner book he sold to Doctor Scott Hall before Brock gets lawyered up. Van writes out his report on the pursuit of Brock and the list of charges he has.

He asks to see the Captain to bring him up to date. After seeing the Captain, Van realizes that he has not eaten all day. He decides to go to his favorite taco stand and eat while Brock thinks of what is in store for him.

THE ARTIMUS BOX

Van takes his time and has a leisurely meal, then he returns to his desk and calls the Santa Monica PD to let them know he has Brock in custody and asks where Doctor Scott Hall is staying. The desk sergeant replies that Doctor Hall is staying at a bed and breakfast in Venice.

Van calls the number that Doctor Hall left with the Santa Monica PD. Doctor Hall answers his cell phone and Van tells him that he has found the man who sold him the book, and that he would like him to come the station and identify him.

Van goes to the holding cells and has Brock moved to an interview room.

Brock is sullen but still defiant.

"You're only going to make things worse with that attitude, Tommy. I told you I can hold you for twenty-four hours without a charge. I've seen really tough guys want to marry Big Al in half that time. It just so happens that Big Al is here with a couple of his pals. He's here on another gang rape charge but he is still a little randy. I told him about you and he's eager to meet you."

"You can't do that. I tell you man, I don't want any part of that."

"Tommy boy, you can tell me what I want to know or I can keep you with Big Al and the boys for as long as I want. I've known of cases where guys like you have been lost in the system for weeks. L.A. County jail system is one of the largest in the world. I can have you moved from one jail to another without anyone but me knowing where you are. Now where did you get the book Tommy? I don't think you're the one who stole it, but I do think you know who did. Talk now or I'll send you to Big Al and I won't be seeing you for a couple of days. You tried to kill me Tommy. You pissed me off big time. If you don't talk now, Big Al can have you and I won't raise a finger to stop him even if you do want to talk."

"I can't tell you man. As soon as I talk I'm a dead man."

"I can protect you here Tommy. No one is going to get at you here."

"You can't protect me man. He's got police in his pocket. He kills guys for the fun of it."

"You know, Tommy, you just gave me a great idea, I'm going to give you to Big Al and tell him that you have been blubbering like a baby. I'm going to tell him you've ratted out everyone you could to save your sorry butt."

"No you can't man, the guy will kill me."

"I don't care Tommy. You think I'm going to waste my time on you, punk? They rape and kill guys like you in here every day. You talk to me now and I can put you in federal witness protection. The man can't get to you there, but you talk to me now or never. I'm going to get some coffee, boy. I'll give you a couple of minutes to think about it."

Leaving another officer to watch Brock, Van leaves the room, slams the door behind him and goes to the front desk.

He asks the desk sergeant if Al Lieber is on duty. The sergeant tells Van that Lieber is on his way back to the station to go off duty. Van asks to have Lieber report to him when he comes in, and goes to get some coffee.

THE ARTIMUS BOX

Unlike most cop shops, this one is small enough that the coffee is really very good. It is the life's blood for many hard working police. This shop makes fresh ground coffee in a gourmet machine the men bought and maintain for themselves. Van is pouring coffee in his own cup when Al Lieber comes in.

"Van, the sarge said you are looking for me."

"You're just the man I need Al. I've got a hard case that won't talk.

I've told him about Big Al and I need you to be him."

"Are we still pulling that old one Van? You know we're not supposed to do that stuff."

"This guy doesn't know the drill Al. He's only been popped for a couple DUI's."

"Okay, I'll get a pair of jail overalls and play the role."

"Just get some pants Al, the grubbier the better. Go in bare-chested, mess up your hair and put on a bunch of cologne. The guy's in interview room 2. I'll give you a cup of coffee to give to the guy. Meet me at the door to the room as soon as you're ready."

Van goes to the interview room and opens the door. Brock slouches over the table and does not look up when Van sits down.

"Okay Tommy boy what's it going to be?"

"I can't man. I can't do it."

"Oh where are my manners? I should have gotten you some coffee Tommy. I'll be right back."

Van goes back out of the room and waits for Al to show up. Al comes down the hall and looks like a huge hairy ape. Van can smell him before Al gets within ten feet of him. "Wow you sure are pretty Al, and you smell so sweet too."

"Yeah, yeah you want me to do this or are you just gonna' have fun?"

"I'm going to have you walk into the room in front of me and then I'm going to leave you with Tommy while you do your boogie man act."

"Let's do it."

Van opens the door. Brock is still looking down at the desk.

"Hey Tommy, Big Al wanted to bring you your coffee himself. Now you two play nice, I'll be back in the morning." Van tells the officer watching Brock to leave. Brock looks up and is startled to see a huge man glowering hungrily at him.

"What, what? Hey, you can't leave me here with him…get him out of here!"

"Tommy just relax boy. I hear it's better that way." Van walks out of the room and turns to close the door.

"Oh no, don't leave, please sir, please," yells Tommy. "I'll tell you his name. Don't go. Really, I'll tell you, you ask me anything, I'll tell you, don't leave me alone. Come on man, make this guy leave, please sir."

"Are you talking to me Tommy? I haven't heard you call me sir before. Why this could be a brand new start for us buddy."

"Yes, sir, I'm talking to you Captain Taylor. I'll tell you whatever you want to know but you have to make this uh, man, go first."

"I'm a detective, Tommy, not a Captain, but I can ask Al to leave. I know he'll be heartbroken, but if your information doesn't pan out you'll be meeting him again."

"Okay, look, I won't lie to you but I need to have protection. The guy told me he can get to me anywhere."

"Al, I'll have to find you someone else. I know how much you wanted to entertain Tommy, but I'll have to take you back to lockup."

Chapter 26

Van returns to the interrogation room and sits down across the table from Brock.

"Okay Tommy, I've wasted all the time I'm going to on you. Give me the name of the person you sold the book for."

"How are going to protect me? I need to know."

"Tommy if I don't hear the name I'm going to send you to Al's cell right now, and I won't come back for you at all."

"Okay man, the guy's name is Dutch, man."

"Dutch? Dutch what, Tommy? What's his last name, where's he live? Get on the bus, boy. I want information."

"I don't know his last name, man. He has some place out in Sunland. He's the leader of a motorcycle gang called Evil's Revenge. The guy's psycho, man. He does crack and steroids and he's crazy with that stuff. He'll kill me if he finds out I ratted him. You gotta protect me man."

"Settle down Tommy. I'm going to run the cycle club's name and see what I find. I'll be back shortly with a mug file so you can identify this Dutch bad boy for me."

THE ARTIMUS BOX

Van goes to his desk computer and first runs the cycle club name; there is a large file with sheets of many arrests for drugs, guns, robbery, and extortions. The name of the leader is Linus Limpter, aka Dutch. Van grins; small wonder the guy has an alias with a name like Linus Limpter.

The rap sheet on Linus Limpter is a long one, and although sentenced to three ten-year terms for drug sales, robbery, and assault, he has only served five years in total. He received early releases from the prisons due to overcrowding of the inmate population. The police arrested Limpter on numerous charges since his time in prison, but he has beaten the charges due to lack of evidence. The witnesses have all gone missing, or have recanted their testimony. The latest mug shots of Limpter show a very large man gone to seed; he does indeed look psycho.

This reminds Van of the man he saw at Phil Manley's shop, the man on the loud motorcycle that threw the pipe. He only got a brief glimpse of the man but enough, with this picture, to know it was the same man.

Van rereads the rap sheet to see if Phil Manley's name comes up. He knows now there is a connection between the Artimus box, Derby, Manley, and the man called Dutch. Van prints out a picture of Dutch and takes it downstairs to Tom Brock.

"Tommy do you know this man?"

"Yes sir that's Dutch. Do you see what I mean about psycho, man? The guy is a nut case. I've heard from his gang buddies that he's killed dozens of guys and buried them in the desert."

"Okay Tom, I'm going to set up a safe house for you until I can get the feds to take care of you. I'm going to have two of my best men to look after you. I'll need your testimony so you can rest easy. I'll make sure you're safe. Do you know a man named Phil Manley, Tom?"

"I don't think so. What does he have to do with this? Is he a gang member?"

"No, Tom, he has a very upscale car restoration shop in Long Beach. I'm pretty sure I saw your friend Dutch there the other day."

"You know I heard some talk about a resto man from the gang guys, something about jobs they were doing for the resto man."

"So, you just hang with the gang guys Tommy, or are you one of them?"

"No man, they come to me to sell stuff for them and threaten me with all kinds of gross stuff. They tell me if I rat, they'll take me out to the desert and rip my skin off one piece at a time. Those guys are scary man; they do that kind of stuff cause they get off on it."

"Can you identify these other gang members Tom? I have a lot of mug shots of Dutch's gang. I know you want to help me on this Tom. It's your only way out. I'm going to send the mug shots with the two officers that are going to take care of you. You look through the pictures and tell the officers what you can about the men you can identify. The last question I have for you is what do you know about the person Dutch has in the police department?"

"All I know is that Dutch and some of the gang brag about having a cop in their pocket."

THE ARTIMUS BOX

"Did they ever say anything that would help us identify the person? Would the person be a detective or a patrolman?"

"No sir, I swear they never said much about it around me. Dutch just told me he had a cop that could put me away if I ever crossed him, or tried to cheat him. He said the cop could find me if I ever tried to run and then he would kill me."

"Did he say the cop was here, in this station?"

"No I don't think so; I think it was like the cop was everywhere."

"Okay Tommy, you keep cooperating with us and I promise to keep you safe from Dutch. If you think of anything that would help me find the rotten cop, call me."

Van leaves Tom Brock in the interview room and goes to the Captain's office to bring him up to date and arrange a safe house for Brock. He assigns Jim and Brad to protect Brock in shifts. The Captain wants to put Al Lieber in with Jim and Brad to lessen the shift hours. Van does not want to use Lieber because, as he explains, he wants to keep Al's randy ape persona intact in case Brock gets cold feet again.

The Captain laughs, "Are you two still using that old gag? You know he could probably walk if you formally charge him. We can't do that stuff now."

"Yes sir, I know, but it still works sometimes. Brock's only been busted for DUI's. He doesn't know from squat, and, you know, that idiot could have killed me today. I wanted some payback. You should've seen his face when I introduced him to Big Al."

The Captain and Van both laugh.

"Yeah I can see it, but don't do it again. If that gets around we'll both be in trouble. Do you get it boyo?"

"Yes sir. I get it Cap; I think I should see Phil Manley to see what he knows about this Dutch character. It seems to me that Manley could be using Dutch to get collections from his customers. On the other hand, it could be that Dutch is using Manley. It looks like Manley's life started to go down hill after Derby was murdered. Maybe Dutch got out of hand and turned the tables on Manley."

"We're spending a lot of time on this, and I'm going to have to go to internal affairs with the bad cop soon. You know I hate those people. I would prefer to find him ourselves."

"I understand Cap; I think Manley is the answer. From what I've read in Dutch's file, we'll have no luck in getting him to talk."

Van tries to phone Manley for two days. He goes to his house and to the Long Beach shop. He cannot find anyone at either place. Van leaves messages on the phone numbers he has for Manley.

In the last message that Van leaves for Manley, he says that he has positive identification on Dutch as the man that stole the Derby/Donner book of drawings. Van tries a bluff, saying that the book ties Dutch to Manley, and that he needs to come in and answer some questions or that he will issue an arrest warrant for him.

Van next goes to records and looks for properties owned by Manley. He cannot find Manley at home or at his business. He must have some place where he stays out of sight. After burning up several hours on the computer, Van has not found any deeds or listed rental agreements.

THE ARTIMUS BOX

Al Lieber sits down at a chair on the other side of Van's desk.

"So how'd you make out with our friend Tommy? Did Big Al win a new admirer?"

"You scared the crap out of him, but then every time I see you I get the same feeling. You fit that Big Al character far too well."

"Oh yeah? You're just a ton of laughs man. As if geezers like you aren't a constant reminder to us young virile studs what the ravages of time will do."

"Jealousy will get you nowhere Al. I age like a fine wine while you, old son, look more the pervert by the day."

"Okay man, enough, I know you've got more than a few rejoinders. So what did you find out?"

"Tommy gave me a guy called Dutch. Get this; his real name is Linus Limpter. He's the leader of a motorcycle gang he calls Evils Revenge. I'm thinking this guy is the heavy in the whole Artimus box case. He apparently has a hangout in Sunland. You were a kid up in the valley. Did you ever hear of this guy or the gang?"

"I know there are some gangs that hang out in Sunland, and some tough guys that the cops up there don't seem to be able to put away. I don't know the big players, it's been too long since I was there. "

"Well I need to talk to this Dutch guy. Do you want to take a ride out to your old stomping grounds with me?"

"I can't right now. I've got to be in court for the next few days, but notify the local cops and have them go with you, Van. They know the lay of the land up there, and some of those gang boys shoot first and they don't ask questions at all. I'm serious Van. Don't go in there alone. Did you find out anything on the inside cop?"

"No, Tommy can't identify the guy, but I will find him or her, you can bet on it."

"Well too bad. But look out for those gang guys; don't go cowboy."

"Okay. Do you know anyone up there that would be a good contact?"

"No, like I said I've pretty much lost track of anyone I knew up there. I think the Captain has some connections up there though."

"Hey, yeah, you're right. I didn't think of that. I'll huddle with Cap first and then run up there and see if I can find this Linus boy. Can you help me find Phil Manley's hideout while you're doing court duty Al? I've looked up property records for other properties he might have in the L.A. area but I can't find any for him other than his house and his shop. I've looked for rentals also."

"Did you look at mobile homes and storage units? He could have something that he used another name to buy or rent. I don't know how we can run that down."

"I didn't run down storage units Al. I agree he could be using an alias but, if he bought or rented in the L.A. area in the last ten years or so, he would have had to complete the legal paperwork. He would need to show good identification. I'm hoping we can find his hideout the easy way. Can you check it out for me?"

"Can do. I can work on that some today before I go to court."

Van enters the Captain's office through the always-open door. The Captain motions him to sit down while he completes a phone call. He hangs up the phone and says, "So boyo, how goes it?"

"I need to locate this Dutch character in Sunland. I need your help in finding a good contact up there to help me find the man. I was talking with Al and he reminded me that you have some in-laws in the police force up there."

"Indeed I do, laddybuck. I know the best man in Sunland, my brother-in-law. Let me give him a call and set something up for you."

Van gets up to leave.

"Sit tight, my boy, I'm going to call my brother-in-law right now."

The Captain phones his brother-in-law and sets up a meeting with Van.

"Okay you can meet him in the morning at the station in Sunland.

"The traffic should be going in the opposite direction from you so the trip shouldn't be so bad. Devin is my brother-in-law and he's a good man with a lot experience in dealing with the gang men up there. He said for you to bring your Kevlar vest. He never goes looking for a gang man without wearing body armor. He knows Dutch and says he's a snake, a very dangerous one. So be very careful Van. Devin would love to be able to put this mutt down for the count, but he hasn't committed any crimes around Sunland that Devin can connect him to."

"Thanks Cap, I'll be careful."

Van signs out an unmarked car and packs his riot gear in the trunk.

Chapter 27

The next morning Van is up and on the road early. His meeting with Chief Devin is at 8:00 am and he wants to be on time. Van drives into Sunland at 7:25 and finds the Police Department. He enters the building and goes to the front desk.

"Good Morning sergeant, I'm detective Taylor. I have an appointment with your chief."

"Yes sir, he is in his office and left word for you to be shown to his office as soon as you arrived. Follow me please."

Van follows the desk sergeant through the modern spotless building to the chief's office.

"Chief, Detective Taylor is here sir."

"Thank you sergeant. Come in. Nice to meet you detective Taylor."

Devin gets up from his chair and reaches his arm out across the desk to shake Van's hand.

Van shakes the chief's hand,"Just Van sir."

"Okay, I'm Devin. I have a few things to do before we can go. We have a small canteen downstairs, you can have some good coffee and pastries if you'd like. I won't be long; I want to get to Dutch before he's too awake."

THE ARTIMUS BOX

"That sounds fine to me Chief Devin. I'll get some coffee and wait for you in the canteen."

After a cup of coffee and a danish pastry, Chief Devin joins Van. The chief is a dark-haired man with the bearing of a tank. He is not tall but very fit; he has a purposeful stride to his walk and exudes a tough confidence.

"I'll join you in a coffee and run down the plan for our meeting with Dutch. I had an officer go by Dutch's place last night to make sure he was there. His bike was there so we assume he is. Mister Limpter is a steroid and crack user; you never know how he'll respond. He apparently got himself in trouble in Columbia some time back. When he got back to the U.S., he was hitting the drugs pretty hard. He can be calm and a wiseass, or totally off the map. If he goes gonzo on us and pulls a gun, he'll use it. Don't hesitate to use force, and I mean deadly force. I won't let him get between us. I don't want you to be alone with him. I don't want to interfere with your job, but I don't want to let the guy have a chance at doing something dumb."

"I appreciate your concern Chief; do you plan on bringing him out in the open to question him?"

"That's the way I've questioned him in the past. That place of his is a rat's nest. I don't think he wants us inside the place either. There's just no telling what he has in there. My understanding is that you just want to question Dutch right now. We'll play it easy this time and not spook him, so just you and I will go. Go get your vest and we can get on the road."

Van and the chief put on their Kevlar vests and get in the chief's four-wheel drive truck for the trip to Dutch's place. They travel down a winding paved road to the pavement's end and then up a dirt road a short distance to a small group of mobile homes and some metal shacks. The mobile homes sit in a U-shape with the metal shacks situated on the outside of the U. The mobiles and the shacks, streaked with rust, stand out ugly against the desert background. There are motorcycles parked in front of the mobiles in various states of repair and trash strewn all about the lot. The chief pulls up to the entrance and shuts off the truck.

"The mobile on the right, with the deck, is Dutch's palace. The thing on the end of the deck is what I presume to be a hot tub. Let me go roust him out."

The chief and Van both get out of the truck. Van stands in front of the truck arms crossed. He watches the chief go up the two steps to Dutch's door. The chief raps on the door and calls out for Dutch to get up and come outside.

"It's Chief Devin, Dutch. Get up and come on outside. I need to ask you some questions."

The chief turns, steps down and rejoins Van at the truck. They wait for Dutch to come out. The door to the mobile bangs open and a very large man steps through the door frame. The man is wearing a leather vest without a shirt and dirty jeans; his upper body is massive. He has long black greasy hair that is as unkempt as the rest of his appearance. His arms are hugely muscled, with prominent blood veins seemingly pulsating. He reminds Van of a caricature of a manic TV wrestler.

"Hey, Dutch, come on down and be sociable. I want to introduce you to my friend, Van. We need to ask you a couple of questions and then we will be on our way."

THE ARTIMUS BOX

"Well, well, Chief Devin, you know it's always a pleasure to see you, man."

Although his voice is controlled and even, his strained body looks as if an invisible leash is holding him back from ripping the world apart.

As soon as Van hears Dutch's voice, he knows he is the man that clubbed him on Sunset Boulevard months ago. He is sure this beast has all the answers he needs to close the Artimus case. Now, how to play him to get the answers, is the question.

"Okay chief, let's meet your buddy, time's money, am I right?"

Dutch comes down the steps and walks to Van. He stops a foot away from Van and glowers down at him. Van does not step back; he moves his hand to shake the hand of the gorilla in front of him. He knows Dutch is going to try to crush his hand if he does shake hands with him. As he expected, Dutch grins and takes Vans hand; his grip is crushing. Van looks into Dutch's eyes as Dutch bears down on his hand. Dutch looks puzzled with the lack of a reaction from Van.

"Hey Dutch, I said I wanted you to meet my friend not make love to him." Dutch drops Van hand and steps back a pace.

"I just wanted to show my good manners Chief. So what can I do for you gents?"

"Dutch, this is Detective Van Taylor from the L.A.P.D. He has the questions for you. Van, Dutch Limpter."

"Just Dutch, chief, you know that. We want to keep this friendly. Am I right?"

"This is all friendly Dutch. Just answer the questions and we can be on our way. I haven't had my breakfast yet."

"Dutch, I'm investigating a robbery and the sale of stolen property. The property in question is a rare book of automotive drawings stolen some ten years ago. The book recently sold to a person from out of town who brought it to the attention of my department. We have information from an informant that you are the man that put the book up for sale."

"Hey man, I look like a book worm to you?"

"No, Dutch, I can honestly say that you do not."

"So, that all man? I got stuff to do."

"Dutch I just have couple more questions. Were you in the employ of a man named Kim Derby ten years ago?"

"Derby? Don't sound familiar man. What's he got to do with anything?"

Van decides to run his bluff. He has no information that places Dutch with Derby. He is not going to get anything out of Dutch without baiting him.

"Well Dutch, Derby was a rich rare car collector who was murdered ten years ago. He had a collection of memorabilia that was much the same as the stolen book. I have information that you knew Derby. That ties you into all of this. You see where this leads us Dutch?"

"You accusing me of something man? I got nothing more to say to you, get the hell out of here."

"Okay, Dutch, if that's the way you want it, I'll just have to get a warrant for suspicion of murder so we can talk downtown."

THE ARTIMUS BOX

"Suspicion of murder? You think I'm that stupid, you jerk? I oughta just pinch your head off, punk."

The Chief moves toward Dutch to stop him from attacking Van, but a man comes from behind and hits Devin on the back with a shovel. There are three men hiding behind one of the mobiles. Two of the men grab Van before he can get his gun out.

"Now I'm gonna pinch your head off smart boy, you been in my way too long. Nobody gets in my way too long, pig boy."

Dutch moves in front of Van and punches him hard in the face. The blow stuns Van to the point of unconsciousness. Dutch steps back and punches him in the stomach as the two men continue to hold Van up.

"Come on Dutch, don't kill a cop man," one of the men holding Van says.

"I'm gonna pinch his head off. I shoulda' killed him when we didn't get the box."

"Come on Dutch, all the cops know where these guys are. We don't got a chance of beating a rap like that. Just calm down, man."

"Who the hell you tell'n to calm down man? I'm just gett'n started."

Chief Devin comes to and reaches for his gun. The third man has a sawed off shot gun that Dutch grabs and fires at the chief. The chief stubbles backward, the shot hits his vest, dust and blood spatters. He falls into a drainage ditch, out of sight. The two men holding Van drop him and run for their motorcycles.

"Hey, where you girls goin'? The fun's just start'n," yells Dutch.

"Dutch, we gotta get out of here man, you killed that cop, man. The pigs'll be all over us."

Van, doubled over on the ground, is trying to get his breath back.

Dutch grabs him by his hair and throws him on his back. Dutch puts his knee in his stomach and with one hand holding the shotgun he puts his other massive hand around Van's neck.

"I told you I was gonna pinch your head off pig boy."

One of the three-gang members has brought his motorcycle up along side Dutch.

"Dutch get a grip man. Let's get out of here. Come on man calm down. We gotta go man."

Dutch has spun completely out of control. He raises the shotgun and blows his gang buddy off his bike. Dutch looks at the gang man on the ground, ignoring the now unconscious Van, he walks over to the downed bike and shuts it off. He stands up and looks around him, dazed and unseeing.

Dutch walks back to his mobile and looks for his crack pipe. He sits down in a chair to light the pipe. Outside the rest of the gang are throwing what valuables they can get on their bikes and leaving the compound. The thundering noise of the motorcycles leaving seems to shake Dutch back to reality. He gets up out of his chair, goes to a trap door under a closet, and removes wads of cash. Dutch grabs a pair of saddlebags, throws some clothes, dope, pills, and the cash in them and goes out the door. He puts the saddlebags on his motorcycle and then returns to his mobile.

Inside the mobile Dutch dumps lighter fluid on the floor. He strikes a match, and as he leaves through the door, he flicks the match back inside, and watches as the floor begins to blaze. Dutch jumps from the deck and fires his motorcycle to life. He roars out of the compound having completely forgotten Van.

Chapter 28

Van wakes to see Chief Devin kneeling beside him with a canteen of water.

"I had to dump half the canteen on you to get you to wake up. You had me worried. Your Captain would have killed me if I let you die out here."

Van sputters back to life and tries to focus on Chief Devin. After some coughing and a long drink of water, he sits up. He is dizzy and not sure if he can stand up.

"Take some time man. You look like crap. Can you breathe? Your whole face is a beet red."

"Give me a minute to get some breath back. Man I thought we were both dead," croaks Van. "I kind of have the impression that my interview technique needs work. Yeah, I know that was dumb, sorry about that. Put it down as a come back from the dead. I'm really glad you're all right. Those guys were waiting for us. Someone set us up."

"No joke, Sherlock. We need to find out whether the louse is yours or mine. I think Dutch is really in bad shape. I knew he was screwed up, but he went off like a firecracker. He killed his own guy over there."

THE ARTIMUS BOX

"Jees, are you okay? I'm just getting my head straight. I saw you get hit and knocked over that little hill. I thought I saw blood fly off your vest."

"I'm hurting man, I don't mind telling you. But most of what you saw was dust on the vest. One of the shot balls caught me under the arm. The blood and dust jumping off my vest when the shot hit me probably saved me from them trying to finish me off. I hit my head on something in that ditch. You've got a huge set of marks around your neck man. Dutch must have tried to strangle you to death."

"I honestly thought I was dead, chief. I couldn't do a damn thing to stop him. I hate to say it, but that guy has more strength in his hands than I do in my whole body."

Devin holds his side. "You know some of the drugs these jerks suck down make them so crazy they think they're invincible. We've had them come at us with axes and clubs after they've tanked up. Two of my men put 14 rounds in one guy and he was still on his feet. They finally brought the guy down with a shotgun but not until he almost chopped my man's arm off. I can tell you, Van, that the next time we meet our friend Dutch, if he makes one bad move we will shoot first. That bum needs to be put down for good."

"Do you have any ideas of where he'll go, chief?"

"I don't know but I am going to find him. As soon as my boys get here and set up a crime scene, we can get out of here. I need some stitches and you need to have some attention. The emergency room is on the way back; let me help you into the truck. I need to call in the whole story to my guys and I'm sure you'll want to call Stoneham."

Van calls in and explains what went down to the Captain. They put out an all points bulletin on Dutch and his gang. The Captain sends two officers out to pick up Van and drive his unmarked back to the department.

"The boys are going to take you home Van. Devin tells me Dutch almost crushed your windpipe. He also tells me someone set you up. We know we have a leak here; we have to shut the rat down now. I hate to bring I.A. into this. But if the guy is in my house, I want to find him.

"I called Kathy. She'll be home when you get there. It was all I could do to keep her from coming up there to get you. I should warn you she's not very happy with you, or me. I thought I could take some of the heat off you by notifying her."

"Thanks Cap. Kathy knows the score. She'll be upset for a bit but she's the strongest woman I've ever known. The doctor gave me a shot of something and some pills to take. My neck is bruised but there's no permanent damage. I'll be in tomorrow and we can make some plans for finding our leak and rounding up Dutch."

"Don't push it, Van. You're no spring chicken. I need you healthy. This stuff can sit a day or two if you need it."

The men drive Van home and walk him to the door of his house.

"Thanks guys, you might want to get out of here before Kathy sees us. I think she may be a little angry. I'll see you guys tomorrow."

Kathy opens the door and stops short of hugging Van.

THE ARTIMUS BOX

"I'm afraid to hug you, you big dummy. Good God you look terrible. I don't want to hurt you. Those bruises on your neck look horrible. What can I do to make you feel better?"

"Um I thought you'd be angry Kathy. Although I have the feeling I still could have some trouble brewing in my future. Is this the calm before the storm?"

"When you're more up to a good chewing out, you can be sure I'll deliver it. You're too old for chasing bad guys by yourself. This is the second time in a week you've come home skinned up, bruised, and half dead. I hate to see you hurt, Van. I don't want you killed. I thought this case was going to be an adventure we could both share but this needs to stop now."

"We can talk about this later Kathy. I'd like to soak in the hot tub and then take a nap."

"I'll go take the cover off the hot tub. Go take your clothes off and come out to the tub. I'm going to watch you and make sure you don't fall asleep in there."

Kathy gets the hot tub ready and helps Van get his clothes off. He puts on a robe, walks out to the tub and Kathy helps him down in the tub. He sits in the hot water and directs the water jets to sooth his neck.

After twenty minutes of relaxing in the tub, Van looks up at Kathy and says, "How about getting us a glass of wine and come get in the tub with me?"

"Oh yeah, look who's Superman now. Come on and let me help you out of the tub and into bed, stud. What you need now is some rest."

"I feel much better now honey, honest. I'll take a little nap and we can have some dinner."

Van gets in bed for his nap. When he wakes up, he sees that Kathy is sitting by a window reading a book.

She looks up at Van and says, "Hey Superman awakens."

"What time is it Kathy?"

"8:30 and that is a.m. not p.m. You've been asleep for twelve hours."

"Jeez, I need to get going, I've got to call the Captain and tell him I'm going to be late."

"I've already called him. He said for you to take the day off. And that is his order too. They haven't found Dutch yet."

"Baby I don't know what I did to deserve you, but the stars were right when I married an angel."

"Go on with you now; you'll make me cry. Don't think I've forgotten to read you the riot act buddy."

Van and Kathy spend the day together and have dinner at a restaurant famous for prime rib overlooking the Santa Monica coastline.

Chapter 29

The next morning, Van is up early, his voice still weak and his body achy, but full of determination to bring the Artimus box case to an end. He is feeling angry and disgusted by Dutch. He is to Van, the lowest kind of criminal. A killer without a conscience, a predator, the kind of psycho that will do anything to get what he wants by walking over anyone he can. Dutch enjoys the pain and suffering he can inflict. Van knows that Chief Devin is right about Dutch, they have to stop him for good.

After arriving at the station house, Van goes directly to the Captain's office. While it is still early morning, the Captain is in his office going through the reports piled on his desk.

"You look like I feel after Saint Paddy's day boyo. Is that a turtle neck sweater or just the color of your neck?"

"I'm happy to see you in such a good mood Cap. Is there any news on Dutch?"

"I have a report here that Phil Manley's place in Long Beach was fire bombed last night. So, I'm thinking Dutch is still around. You said you thought it was Dutch, that threw the pipe through the front of

Manley's place. I have the feeling he's ramping up the urgency of his last message."

The Captain's intercom sounds and the Captain lifts the receiver to his ear.

"Okay sergeant put him through to me." The Captain listens to the person on his phone. After some time he speaks into the phone, "I'm sending officers to your location to bring you to this station, give me your address.

"That was Phil Manley. He's in full panic mode. He's received numerous phone messages from Dutch. His house has also been fire bombed. Apparently Dutch said in one of his messages that you told him Manley had ratted him out just before he killed you. He's threatening to kill Manley now. He wants protection.

"I'm sending a patrol unit to pick him up. When we have him here, we can tell him to give us all he knows about the whole Artimus box affair in exchange for his protection. I want you to interview him and keep the pressure on him until we have the answers to this case. I want this wrapped up without any more blood shed. We need to find Dutch and our rat. Let's get them both in a cell in this station a.s.a.p.

"Find out how Dutch wants Manley to contact him. Maybe we can nail down his location that way. If we can gain access to a cell phone number Dutch is using we can track him down when he uses it."

"Captain I'm going to check duty records, and cell phone records for our own personnel. I want to see if they might tie into any of the times we've had information leaks. That should keep me busy until Manley is brought in."

THE ARTIMUS BOX

"That's a real long shot, but still well worth checking. I'll have Manley taken to the interview room when he gets here. I'll call you in the records room then."

"Okay Cap."

Van is back in the records room doing more of what he describes as ass-burn work. Almost anything to do with paper work is a pain for him. Van likes to be out on the streets where the crimes are. The paperwork required for modern day reports is daunting.

He is not finding anything that he thinks will lead him to the department's information leak. Van is relieved when the Captain calls him to say that Manley is in the interview room. When Van enters the interview room, Manley is in a chair with his head in his hands. He looks up as Van comes through the doorway.

"My God it's you, I thought you were dead."

"No, Phil, although your friend Dutch did try his best, I'm still with the living. We haven't been able to locate Dutch but I'm depending on you to help us find him."

"I need protection from Dutch because of you. You told Dutch that I ratted him out; now he's going to kill me."

"I didn't tell Dutch that you gave him up Phil. The guy is so flipped out he can't think straight. He's been on his drug cocktail mixture for too many years.

But I want you to understand right now that if you don't cooperate and tell me everything I need to know, I'll put you out on the street. It just might be that using you for bait would be the best way to get Dutch anyway."

"No you can't do that. You're a police officer, you can't put me out."

"Manley, you have no idea what I can or will do. I promise you if you don't tell me the truth, I'll drive you to your Long Beach shop and throw you out of my car. Now no more stalling, how do you get in touch with Dutch?"

"He's been calling me; I have two numbers for him. You can try them if you want. He's set fire to the shop and my house. I don't know if the phones work at either place. I'm not going to stay at either place to wait for him to call or come by and kill me."

"Phil, have you tried the phone numbers you have for Dutch?"

"I tried to call him last night. I wanted him to know I didn't rat on him. The home number I have for Dutch is out of service and the cell number I have just rang with no answer."

Van writes the numbers down and tears the numbers from his note pad. He has an officer take the numbers to have them checked out. "I'm going to have the numbers checked right now," he tells Manley.

"Now Phil, let's start with the Derby murder. That's what set Dutch off when I asked him about it. How are you involved with Kim Derby's death? Give it up right now. Don't think about some story line, and don't lie about it, talk now."

"I have to know how you're going to protect me first. Dutch has someone in this department that feeds him information. He'll know I'm here. I need to get out of the country, somewhere safe. What are you going to do about keeping me safe?"

"Who does he have in this department?"

THE ARTIMUS BOX

"I don't know but I can't trust anybody here, I know that."

"I have officers I can trust Phil. We can go to the Federal Marshall's for your protection, but only after you hold up your end. What happened with Kim Derby? Don't lie to me. Talk now or I'm going to handcuff you and take you to Long Beach right now. I'll find Dutch when he finds you."

"Okay, okay, I'll tell you. All you big bastards have to show how tough you are. I hate you Neanderthals pushing me around all the time. All right, I'm getting to it. I met Dutch a long time ago. The motorcycle group he was with was doing security at rock concerts and big charity events. I asked him to help with car parking and security at an event in Palm Springs that I was putting on. The year before some college kids on spring break crashed the gate and damaged some of the members' cars that were on display. The college kids were drunk or drugged or both, and out of control. We needed help to keep our members and the cars safe. Dutch brought some of his men and they really looked mean. We had no trouble from the college kids and we used his men for a few years for security.

"Dutch would come by my shop and was very interested in the cars I had and the work we did on them. He was always a tough guy but I thought I could handle him or a least reason with him."

"Let's get to Kim Derby Phil. You're stalling, come on what happened there?"

"I just wanted to give you the whole picture, I'm not the bad guy here you know. I was doing all of Kim's restoration work. We were friends. He decided to sell most of his cars, but he wanted to keep the Artimus memorabilia he had collected. Kim bought the property that Harry Artimus had his ranch on. He wanted to tear down some of the old buildings that were beyond repair. He wanted a crew of men he could trust because he thought that there could be things of value in the place. I set him up with Dutch and some of his guys.

"Kim called on the day of his murder. He said he was feeling uneasy about Dutch. I told Kim I would call Dutch and get things straightened out. The next day I heard about Kim's murder, I didn't have any idea Dutch would do anything to hurt Kim."

"Did you call Dutch? Did you tell the police about Kim Derby's phone call to you? You could have placed Dutch at the Derby house at the time of the murder."

"Well, ah, Dutch was the person who told me of Kim's death. He said he'd kill my whole family and me if I told the police. I've been living in hell since that day."

"You're telling me that for over ten years you've withheld evidence in a murder case that could have put Dutch in prison?"

"Can't you see? He would've killed me. I had no choice."

"What I can see, is that you aren't telling me the whole story. What happened to the Artimus memorabilia that Derby collected? We know someone took it from the house before the fire broke out. We know that someone deliberately set the fire to cover up the murder and robbery.

"So what I'm seeing, is that you sent Dutch to kill your friend Kim Derby. You wanted the Artimus stuff yourself. Isn't that the way it happened? Dutch has some of the Artimus stuff he stole. We know that because we have a witness. Where is the rest of it Phil? If the rest of the stuff is where Dutch can get it, we can stake it out and grab him when he tries to get it."

"I don't know where the stuff is. I had nothing to do with Kim's murder. I just want this nightmare to be over. I haven't done anything wrong."

"You're not telling me the whole truth. If Dutch wants to kill your whole family, why aren't you concerned with their safety?"

"My wife divorced me. She took the kids and left. You know that."

"I do know that, Phil. So, you are not concerned that Dutch will harm your family. You're just afraid that Dutch will kill you. You're telling me that for ten years you haven't said anything because Dutch threatened you. You know, you don't spin a very convincing story. I think you helped Dutch. I think you're in this whole mess with Dutch. I don't know whether to pitch you out on the street or charge you with murder and robbery."

"If you don't want to believe me, then I don't have any faith that you'll protect me. You can't charge me with anything. I haven't done anything wrong. I'm going to get out of here. I need to be safe."

"Okay Phil, if you think you will be more safe on the outside, you can go for now. Don't leave the city without telling me. If I can't find you, I will issue a warrant for your arrest. Where are you staying?"

"I'm not going to tell you. I'll give a phone number where you can contact me. I'll let you know if I have to leave."

"I'm going to ask you one more time Phil. Where is Dutch?"

"I don't know. I hope you find him before he kills me. If I knew where he was I would tell you."

"That is the only part of your story I believe Phil. You understand if you leave here I can't protect you?"

"I have to protect myself. You don't care if I live or die; you just want Dutch because he tried to kill you."

"What I want, Phil, is the truth. You give me that and I'll help you as much as I can.

We can make a deal with the D.A. if you agree to tell the whole story. I will get Dutch one way or another. He has killed without a thought or care and he will keep on killing until I put him away. He's like a rabid dog; he won't stop until he's put down for good."

Phil gets up out of the chair and sullenly walks out of the door. Van follows Manley out of the room. When Manley calls a cab, Van runs to find Al Lieber in the squad room.

"Al, I want you to follow Phil Manley. I want to know where he's staying. Don't let him know he's being followed, and be on the lookout for Dutch. I don't know if Dutch knows where Manley's hiding out. I don't think Manley would leave here if he thought Dutch could find him."

Al changes into street clothes and waits for Manley's taxi to pick him up. The cab arrives and Phil Manley gets in. They drive off with Al staying just in sight of the cab.

They head east on the Santa Monica freeway for miles and turn south on the 710 freeway. They get off the freeway on Firestone and head east again. A mile east of the freeway, the cab stops in a gas station. Manley gets out and pays the cab driver. Al continues past the gas station and turns into a Quick Mart. Al gets out of his car and locks it.

He walks back toward the gas station. Manley is walking toward Al down the sidewalk.

Al turns left up an alley to avoid him and keeps walking. Manley walks by without looking in the alley, he is busy watching behind him.

There are very few people on the sidewalk. L.A. is not a city of heavy foot traffic. Al does not want to try and follow Manley in his car, but following him on foot and not have Manley spot him will be tough. Al decides to stay off the sidewalk. Instead, he will stay close to the storefronts. Manley walks twenty or thirty yards and then turns around to look behind him.

Al pulls a ball cap from his pocket and puts it on. As he follows he notes that Manley travels about the same distance every time before he turns to look behind him. Al can now make himself invisible to Manley by blending into the background as Manley turns to survey behind him.

Al still takes the precaution to take off his shirt, so that he is now wearing a tee shirt. He alternates his appearance by changing his shirt, taking it off, and putting on his hat.

Manley continues down Firestone for ten blocks. He turns to his right and goes into an alley; he stays in the alley for eight blocks before turning to his left. Al is being very cautious now. He is easy for Manley to spot in an alley. Manley is still keeping to his routine of turning to look behind him at the same intervals. Manley is walking through alleys. He is turning right, left, and looking behind him. After twenty minutes of walking, he comes to a gated storage lot. He takes a card from his wallet and inserts it in a box by the gate.

The gate opens and he walks into the lot. Manley waits for the gate to close before he moves deeper into the lot.

Al moves quickly to the lot.

As he approaches the gate, a pick up truck drives up to the entrance and the driver inserts his card to open the gate. When the gate opens, Al walks in beside the truck, keeping to the blind spot of the driver's view.

Al walks toward the last place he saw Manley go. At the end of each row of storage units is a big round curved mirror. Al quickly walks to each mirror and looks down each row using the mirrors to see down the rows without Manley spotting him.

Four rows down, Al can see Manley entering a unit that has a roll up door and a man door beside it. Manley is using a key to open the man door. Al waits for him to go into the unit.

He sees him go in the door. Before closing the door, Manley turns and looks up and down the row. Al uses the mirror to watch him. He again stays at an angle to the mirror, this keeps Manley from seeing him. Al makes note of the unit number and dials his cell phone.

THE ARTIMUS BOX

Chapter 30

Van goes back to running the duty records trying to find their bad cop. The long shots sometimes do bring results. Van's phone rings and Al gives him the address of the storage unit Manley is using.

"We need to get a search warrant for that unit Al. Come on back to the station and I'll get to work on the warrant. Tomorrow we'll pay Mister Manley a visit. I'm willing to bet we find what is left of Derby's treasure in that storage unit."

As night falls, Phil Manley is sitting in his storage unit drinking vodka out of the bottle. He has been crying. There does not seem to be any way out, his life is in ruin. He knows that either Dutch will kill him or he is going to prison for his part in Kim Derby's murder. He feels the grip of Van Taylor is closing in on him. In the still gloom of his tiny storage unit world, surrounded by his treasures, he is thinking of suicide. Maybe that's the best way out.

He shakes out of the gloom, when hears some movement outside the unit. With the weariness of a broken old man, he gets up again to make sure the locks are set on the doors. Manley presses his ear to the door, the noise he heard is gone. He turns to go back to his chair and sees water running under the roll up door. Manley uncoils from the old man posture and quickly goes back to the door to unlock the dead bolts. As the last dead bolt unlocks, a force violently pulls the door open from the outside. Manley steps back as Dutch steps in and without a word stabs Manley in the stomach with a huge knife. Dutch holds the knife in Manley's stomach as Manley sinks to the floor in shock.

"Hold that knife in your belly Phil boy; I don't want you to bleed out while I load all this stuff in the van. Watch me take all your stuff. When I finish loading I'm gonna finish you too."

"I didn't tell on you. Holy Jesus, get me to a hospital. Don't let me die. Oh, god I can't stand this, sweet Jesus it hurts. This is all that lousy cop Taylor's fault. Help me Dutch, don't let me die, it's Taylor you want."

"Oh yeah, Manley, I'm going to help you. I'm gonna to twist the knife you're holding on to and make you scream like a little girl. Yeah I'm going to enjoy that Philly. And right after I finish with you I'm gonna waste all the bastards that have been screwing with me. I'll take care of Taylor too. I got big plans for Van the dip shit, man."

"I'm gonna to go get Taylor's little woman and take her somewhere that I can spend some time enjoying her. Then I'm going to invite Van, "the superman", Taylor to come watch me play with her. After I finish I'm gonna kill both of them real slow. Now don't go nodding off on me, Phil old buddy."

After Dutch turns off the water hose, he opens the back doors of the van and throws the entire contents of

THE ARTIMUS BOX

Manley's storage unit into the back. Not taking time to pack or preserve anything, he stuffs everything in the van. Dutch shatters the glass cabinets Manley had installed to hold his treasures.

The glass in the picture frames shatter as he throws them in a heap. Dutch is raging again. Any physical activity now seems to trigger the steroids. Bookbindings are torn and papers scattered. He slams the rear doors of the van shut, and walks over to Manley.

"You miserable little bastard, I told you to wait for me."

Dutch is yelling at a very dead Phil Manley. He pulls the knife out of the body and repeatedly slashes Phil's head and neck with the huge knife.

Dutch wipes the blood from the knife blade on the remains of Manley's shirt. He opens the door and looks outside. With the coast clear, he opens the roll up door and drives the van out of the unit into the alley. He returns to the storage unit to close and lock the doors, and then drives off.

His next stop is in Santa Monica to catch Kathy Taylor as she closes her shop for the night.

He blasts through traffic across the freeways and on to surface streets. Dutch parks the van across the street from Kathy's shop. He does not have to wait long. Kathy locks the door of her shop and walks down the street toward the parking garage. Dutch turns the van around and crosses the street behind her as she enters the parking garage.

The garage is a multi-level concrete structure. At this late hour, most of the patrons have picked up their cars and left for the day. Kathy parked her car in her designated space toward the back of the first level.

As she opens her purse for her car keys, Dutch drives the van behind her and stomps on the brakes. The tires scream on the concrete floor. Startled, Kathy turns to see an ugly giant rushing toward her with a huge knife in his fist.

Before she can utter a scream, Dutch clubs her with the butt of the knife and grabs her before she hits the ground. He opens the rear doors of the van and throws Kathy on top of the pile of stuff. Dutch jumps in the van and drives deeper into the garage. He backs in a dark corner and goes to the rear of the van. Dutch opens the rear doors and looks at Kathy as she lies unconscious in the pile of Artimus treasures.

He wants to hurt her, to humiliate her, to show her his great power. But not here, somewhere with no one around where he can do anything he wants for as long as he wants.

For the first time Dutch tries to think of where he is going to hold up, a place he can hide and take care of the revenge he wants to reap. He pulls a roll of duct tape from the front of the van and wraps Kathy's arms and legs. He runs his big hands over her body and up her skirt, he is breathing hard.

Dutch moves his hand across her lips and Kathy suddenly comes to life and clamps down on his fingers with her teeth. Dutch yanks his torn bleeding finger from her mouth. Kathy yells at Dutch.

"Get off me you fat stinking ape."

Dutch grabs the roll of duct tape and as Kathy struggles against him, he covers her mouth.

THE ARTIMUS BOX

"That will hold you for now, you little bitch. You're a real little tigress. Well baby that's just the way I like'em. You like to scratch and bite, you like it rough yeah that's what you want. Well big Dutch is gonna to make you wait for me till I get you to a safe place baby. Then I'll knock you around a little, show you some rough, yeah baby."

Dutch gets out of the back and slams the doors. He gets behind the steering wheel and starts the van.

His bleeding finger is making the steering wheel slick. Grabbing the duct tape Dutch winds the tape around his finger. He hears a motorcycle coming down from an upper level of the garage with a very distinctive sound. The motorcycle comes down the ramp and turns in front of the van, headed out to the exit. It is a beautiful vintage Vincent Black Shadow.

Dutch looks at the motorcycle and tries to place where he has seen one like it. The machine makes him think of a place he would be safe. Years before, he picked up a Black Shadow for Phil Manley. One of Manley's automotive restoration customers owned the bike. Manley sent it to a man that specialized in early motorcycles in Twentynine Palms to do the restoration. Dutch had been back to the place a number of times since. The last time he rode out to the place, the owner of the shop said that he was going to retire and close the shop. The shop was in a deserted canyon near a dry lake. Dutch starts the van and heads out to the desert. A wide grin spreads on his ugly face; he has the perfect place. No one is going to be able to find him out there. He can be safe there for as long as he wants.

It takes Dutch almost four hours to get to the place. It has become a pitch-dark moonless night by the time he turns on the dirt road to the canyon. He drives up the canyon road several miles to a small road leading to the shop. Nestled in the rock and cactus is a large corrugated sheet metal building. The flat roof is grown over with dirt and cactus for insulation from the blistering hot days and cold nights. A small adobe house is set twenty yards off to the side of the building with old trees and shrubs situated around it.

Outside lights go on and a stringy old white haired man comes out of the house carrying a shotgun.

"Get out of here. Turn that thing around and drive it off of my property," the old man says.

Dutch gets out of the van with his hands up.

"Hey Gus, it's me Dutch. I got some car trouble. Can you help me out, man?"

"Dutch, what in the hell are you doing out here at this time of night?"

"I gotta bike I want you to look at man. I'm driving out here in all this traffic and it's getting' late man. Now this stinkin' van is goin belly up on me. It took me a lot longer to get here than I thought it would."

"Dutch, I haven't seen you in years. You come way out here without calling first. How'd you know I'm still here?"

"Gus you told me your kin's been living out here since the eighteen hundreds. Where you gonna go man?"

"Okay Dutch, I'll take a look at your bike, then you gotta go. I need my beauty sleep."

Gus walks toward the back of the van. Dutch moves in front of the old man to block his view.

"Hey Gus, can I get a crescent wrench and screwdriver first? I need to tighten the fan belt on this piece of junk. The alternator light is coming on and it's overheating."

"I have to get my keys to the shop from the house. Wait out here."

Gus goes in his house and comes back out with a key ring. He has left his shotgun in the house. Dutch follows Gus to the shop as he unlocks the shop door.

"Gus, you still out here with no one to look out for you man?"

"I don't need looking after Dutch."

"Gee that's too bad, Gus."

Gus has his back to Dutch as he goes into the shop and turns on the lights. Dutch pulls out his big knife and grabs the old man by the hair on his head. He pulls the knife across the old man's throat.

Dutch picks up the frail man's body and takes him back out of the building. He carries the man to a dry creek bed behind the building and drops the body. A cloud of dust raises as the lifeless body hits the creek bed.

Dutch walks back to the van and picks up a struggling Kathy. He carries her into the house to the one bedroom and dumps her on the bed. Her bruised face contorted with both pain, and anger, Kathy's eyes flare with revulsion.

Dutch stands over her with his shirt bloodied from the two murders he has done today. His long greasy hair is matted, his ugly face spattered with blood and dirt.

"When I'm finished with you, you're gonna have bruises all over that pretty little body of yours, baby. I'm gonna call your old man and get him out here so he can watch. I'm gonna pinch his head off right in front of you so you can watch too. How's that sound to you baby, that gonna be rough enough? I gotta go back and get my cycle from Downey before some joker steals it. I'm gonna tape you down so you can't go nowhere.

"You oughta get some sleep. You're gonna need all your energy for big Dutch baby, I'll be back in the morning."

After duct taping Kathy to the bed, Dutch goes out to the van and backs it up to the shop's big main door. He opens the door and backs the van inside the shop. From the back of the van, he pushes all the stuff he took from Manley's storage unit out on to the floor of the shop.

The shop is clean and bright. Along the ceiling of the shop is a system of pulleys and belts. The big leather belts that run from the ceiling pulleys go to each machine to run the many machines in the shop. Machine shops used this type of system in the late eighteen hundreds. Gus had kept the machines and the system in top working condition all these years.

His work restoring early twentieth century motorcycles earned him worldwide appreciation. His shop was the envy of most of his clientele. Even though Gus was retired, many people offered outrageous sums of money for him to work on their machines.

Dutch pulls the van out and gets out, closing the shop door. He gets back in and starts his trip back to Downey to pick up his motorcycle. Dutch smiles to himself, he thinks he has the world in his fist for the taking.

The devil goes about his work.

Chapter 31

When Van gets home after work, Kathy is not home yet, but she always calls if she is going to be very late. Van orders some tacos and chili rellenos from the local Mexican food place and asks to have them delivered. He goes to the refrigerator to get a cold bottle of Tecate beer. After the food arrives, he puts the food in the oven to stay warm and calls Kathy's cell number. The phone rings without answer. He calls her shop phone, the answering machine clicks on with her after hours message.

Van calls the car company's number for Kathy's Cadillac CTS. He identifies himself as the owner of the car, and asks that they track the car with their satellite GPS system. They tell Van that the car is still at the parking lot by Kathy's shop. Van is up all night phoning hospitals and ambulance companies. He calls the Captain and tells him Kathy is not home and he cannot find any trace of her.

"I have a bad feeling, Cap. I think Dutch grabbed her. He said he would that time he attacked me."

"Don't get over centered, Van. We will find her. You stay by a phone and I promise I'll put the whole department on finding her."

"I just can't sit here Cap, I'll go nuts, I need to get that search warrant for Manley's storage unit and get him to tell me where Dutch is hiding."

"Okay, come to the station and I'll meet you there with the warrant. I have to go wake up a judge I know to get it signed. I want you to call Al and have him go with you. I know what this means to you, but you can't beat an answer out of Manley. I want a witness on site with you, do you understand? I'm going to have the local cops there too."

"I get it Cap. You're right, I'd like to beat it out of Manley. He's been the instigator of this whole deal with Dutch. All he can say for himself is that nothing is his fault. I'm going to call Al now and get on my way. I'll see you at the station."

Van meets Al Lieber at the station. They get the completed warrant from the Captain and head for Downey to get into Manley's storage unit.

The early morning traffic is bad; the freeway is stop and go. Van gets off the freeway and travels the surface roads. The traffic on the surface roads is not moving much faster than the freeway. Van pounds the steering wheel and yells at the traffic.

"Take it easy, Van we'll get there. Why don't you let me drive?"

"I can't sit still Al, these idiots just need to concentrate on driving. These nuts are drinking coffee, putting on their make up, or texting on their phones instead of watching the road. If half of these idiots would concentrate on the road, traffic in this city would move instead of being a parking lot."

"That's all true, but busting a gut isn't going to get us there any faster."

THE ARTIMUS BOX

"I'm going to get off Firestone and take a side street; one of these streets has to move faster than this."

After what seems to take an eternity, Al and Van arrive at the storage facility. The Captain called the owner of the place and has him standing by to open the front gate. They identify themselves to the man at the gate and drive to Manley's unit. Van gets out of the car and beats on the door of Manley's unit.

"He's not going to open the door. I don't hear any movement inside. Get the bolt cutters Al. The man-door has a dead bolt inside but the roll up just has a padlock. We can cut the shackle off."

Al takes a bolt cutter from the trunk of the car and snaps the lock. Van turns the handle in the center of the door and pulls the door up.

At first in the dim light, it looks like the unit is empty inside. Van looks for a light switch, finding it on the door jam, flips it up. The overhead lights blink to life and as Van turns to look to the back of the unit, he almost trips over Manley's body slumped against the wall.

"Damn it, damn it, damn it, this has got to be Dutch's work. Manley, you poor dumb idiot, you knew Dutch would get you. Now you're useless to me."

"Al, we need to go through the stuff on the floor. Maybe he left something we can use. I'm going to go through his pockets before the locals get here."

Van finds Manley's wallet, keys and personal belongings in his pants' pockets. He finds a small cell phone in Manley's shirt pocket.

Van goes to the address section of the phone and finds a number for Dutch. He dials the phone thinking that it could not be this simple.

"Yeah who the hell is this? It sure ain't my old buddy, Phil Manley."

"Thanks for the confession, Dutch. I didn't think you were bright enough to use caller identification."

"Well, well, well, if it ain't the little super hero. I was just gonna call you man. I guess I musta forgot to call sooner. I been having so much fun with your little woman."

"Dutch, if you hurt her I'll kill you. No, on second thought, why don't we meet somewhere just you and me. You think you can take me. I hear you 'roid user's can't get it up anyway. Maybe that's your problem Linus, you a little limp boy?

"Oh, my, am I scared? Look pig, I'm more man than you'll ever be. I've knocked you down easy every time, you ain't got nothing for me. Now get me that box and you can come watch me with your old lady. I promise you a real fun time."

"Where are you Dutch?"

"You just get me that box. Keep hold of that phone and I'll call you with the time and place little man. I gotta get back to your sweet little woman. I know she's miss'n me."

Dutch closes the connection, and Van redials., There is no answer.

"Van we should have set up a trace before you called him."

"Sweet Jesus, man, don't you think I know that. I really didn't think he'd answer the phone. We'll have to set up a trace when I have the box ready for him. I just pray he hasn't hurt Kathy. I've got to get him. I've got to find Kathy."

THE ARTIMUS BOX

"As soon as we get back to the station Van, I'll get busy trying to round up some of Dutch's gang. Maybe we can find where he has Kathy."

Van and Al turn the crime scene over to the local police, and return to their station house. On the way, Van calls the Captain and reports the latest events.

"Van the local cops are angry that you left the crime scene so fast. They weren't able to get all the information they need to start their investigation properly.

I told them that you have an emergency and we will give them a full report and access to all of our investigation. I've asked the bank manager to bring me the contents of the safety deposit box and sent our key. I'm going to have the diamonds marked by the guy the robbery squad uses. We'll have everything ready by the time you get back here."

"Cap, I really don't give a damn about their investigation. All I care about right now is Kathy. He's got her. We need to be set up and ready to receive Dutch's phone call. I want to be able to trace it whether it's a cell or land line call. I've got to get to Kathy before he can hurt her. I can't let that happen."

"I'm on it Van, we have the whole place working for you. We'll get Kathy back safely, Van, you have to believe that."

"What I know is that Dutch is a psycho. All I know is I have to get to him before he can hurt Kathy."

Van and Al drive back to the station. The traffic is lighter and they make good time.

Van is in a black mood. Al tries to lighten the mood, but Van will have none of it. Al fidgets in his seat, he looks out the car door window at the other cars and steals glances at Van who is staring stonily straight out in front of the car.

They reach the station house and Al jumps quickly out of the car. He shouts to Van over his shoulder that he is off to get after his contacts and try to locate Dutch. Van says, "Yeah, you do that," in reply and storms up to the Captain's office.

"Van I'm glad you're back. Come in and have a seat. I just talked to the man we had mark the diamonds. After all this trouble over the damned box, the stones are fake, they're glass. The man said they're first class fakes, and from the way they were polished, he thinks they are seventy to a hundred years old. I put the fake diamonds in a pouch and stuck it in the box. The property clerk has the box, it's ready to go. We have to sign it out to use it as bait."

"Cap listen, before we get into all that we need to keep an eye on Al. I can barely think straight, but it's got to be him."

"Al Lieber? Why? What's going on? Are you thinking he's our rat?"

"It all comes down to him Cap. Dutch killed Manley last night. Al was the only man outside you and me that knew where Manley was. I hate to be right but it has to be Al. He wasn't surprised to see Manley dead. He was angry, but I think that was because he didn't think Dutch would be so stupid as to kill Manley last night. Al's smart enough to know that he's made. We need to watch him. He must know where Dutch is."

"You make it sound right, but why would he do it? He's your friend, he loves you and Kathy. You can't just turn that on and off. He's been a good cop, his record is flawless. I don't understand what he would have to gain. Man, I hope you're wrong Van, but by god, if he's dirty I won't have it. I'll make him stand trial for it. His wife and kids will have a hard time with this. If he's dirty, Van, I want to know why."

Chapter 32

The Captain calls the front desk and tells the sergeant to find Al Lieber right now and report back to him. Within minutes the desk sergeant calls back, to report that Al did not check in with him. He asked one of the men in the squad room if he had seen Al. The man said he saw Al go to the property clerk and try to sign out the box and jewels. He told the property man that the Captain sent him to get it. The clerk told Al he needed the Captain's signature before he could release the box. Al just turned around, ran straight through the station, and took off in his own car.

Van calls Al's cell phone and gets a busy signal.

"Captain, can we break into Al's call?"

"Let me call the phone company and set it up."

Van paces back and forth across the room while the Captain calls the phone company.

"Okay, the phone company says that when they broke into the call the party that Al was speaking to broke off. Al told the phone company that he'll call here in an hour."

"An hour, is he nuts Cap? I want to find Kathy. Doesn't he care? This is his doing. I could kill him for this. If he knows where Kathy is, and anything happens

THE ARTIMUS BOX

to her, I'll kill him I swear to God. There's no telling what that monster could do to Kathy in an hour. Al must have gone stupid, or maybe he's in with Dutch on this whole deal.

Damn him, I'll kill both of them."

"Get a hold of yourself man, I'll put you in a cell if you can't use your head and get yourself under control. I'm serious Van, you listen to me. Start thinking like a cop right now. You know how this has to go. I can't let you loose if you're going to go to pieces. The way you're thinking could get you and Kathy both killed."

"Okay, okay, you're right. I know you're right, Cap. This is tearing me up, I just can't stand the thought of that animal with Kathy, but I can keep it together. I'm all right. I won't do anything stupid."

"Okay then, Van. I'll have the desk sergeant keep calling his number. Maybe he'll come to his senses or get tired of having the phone ring."

"Can we find his location by calling his number Cap?"

"I'll find out from the phone company what they can do."

After what seems hours to Van the Captain hangs up the phone. "The phone company is setting it up. It may take a while."

Twenty minutes later the Captain's intercom buzzes.

"The desk sergeant says Al is answering his phone, he wants to talk to you."

"Al where is Dutch? I don't care about anything right now except finding Kathy before Dutch hurts her."

"I'm so sorry, Van; I never thought anything like this would happen. I promise I'll call you when I get to where Dutch is. I'll make sure Kathy is safe, and then I'm going to kill Dutch."

Van covers the speaker on his phone, and asks the Captain to trace the call while he keeps Al on the line.

"Al, you dumb son of a bitch, tell me where you're going now! What if Dutch kills you? You think of that? What if you can't help Kathy? Come on Al don't make this worse. We've been friends for a long time. I know you love Kathy. You don't want to see her hurt."

"Please believe me Van. I'm really sorry about this mess; but, I have to do this my way. I screwed this whole thing up; I should have come to the Captain and you in the beginning. It just kept getting worse and I kept getting in deeper and deeper."

"Good God man, why in the hell would you put in with Dutch? How could you let him take Kathy? I can't figure it out."

"Please, Van, let me try to explain. I went to high school with Dutch up in Devonshire. We were in a gang of kids together before Dutch flunked out. Dutch was wild and dumb even then. We went in a liquor store one night to try to get some beer. We were both under age, and Dutch thought he looked old enough to get the beer. We got a couple of six packs, and went to the counter to pay for them. The man behind the counter wanted to see some I.D. Dutch took a gun from his jacket and told the counterman to give him all the cash out of the register.

"The guy behind the counter just got mad and told Dutch to go to hell. Dutch put the gun against the guy's chest. The man said, "Don't be dumb, kid, put the gun away." He said he wouldn't call the cops.

Dutch just laughed and shot him in the chest and went behind the counter to take the money. The poor guy was on the floor moaning.

"Dutch couldn't get the register opened so he tells the guy to get up and open the cash register drawer. The guy couldn't get up so Dutch shot the guy again. I just stood there. I couldn't believe it was happening, I couldn't even move.

"Dutch threw the gun to me and told me to put it in my pocket while he broke open the register. I put the gun in my pocket and ran outside. I didn't know what to do. Dutch came out of the place and told me to give him back the gun. He held out the bag he put the money from the register in, and I dropped the gun in the bag. I told Dutch I never wanted to see him again, and ran home. I didn't tell anybody about it.

"A couple of days after the robbery, Dutch found me after school. He told me that if I ever told anyone about the robbery and killing, he would say that I killed the counterman. He said he had the gun he used, and it had my fingerprints on it. The fingerprints would prove I killed the man. I didn't see Dutch for ten or twelve years. The death of the liquor store man has always troubled me, but I didn't ever do anything about it."

The Captain has been listening in on the call with Van. He motions to Van to cover the phone receiver.

"He's headed east on the 10 freeway. He's already past Ontario; he must be flying. Keep him talking."

"Are you tracking me Van?"

"I am doing everything I can think of to find Kathy, Al, and if that means running you to ground, you know I'll do it."

"I have to square this Van. I'll get Kathy out, believe me. She comes first."

"How did Dutch find out about the Artimus box Al? You must have told him."

"I did. That jerk showed up at my house one night and scared my wife out of three years' growth. He tells me he is so sorry for the past and he wants to make up for it. Dutch says that Phil Manley had killed some guy years ago and that he wanted to clear himself of any charges that might come from that.

He said that Manley stole a bunch of Artimus stuff from the guy's house and was trying to find a box that went with the Artimus stuff.

Dutch said he read in the paper that a construction crew found a body buried with a wooden box. I don't know how he knew it was the Artimus box. Dutch claimed he could prove that he had nothing to do with the guy Manley killed. All he needed to do was to get the box. Dutch told me he could clear himself of that murder and he'd turn himself in on the liquor store killing. I was the one that told him you had the box."

"Did you really believe that after all the years gone by that Dutch would turn himself in, Al?"

"I guess I just wanted to believe he was telling the truth. Dutch was never bright, but he is cunning. After he attacked you, I told him I was turning him in. He said that you were trying to pull your gun and one of the guys he had with him hit you. I told him I didn't care, I was still done with him. He said he still had the gun that killed the liquor store man and that now he could tell the police that I had been giving out confidential police information. He said with me in jail there would be no one to protect my wife and kids.

"Dutch said he could hide out in South America with some drug buddies of his until the heat was off here. Then he'd come back and take care of my family. He and his buddies are stone killers. I knew they'd do it. I know I should have stopped there but Dutch would have framed me and killed my family. You know he would, Van. I've got to make this right; there's only one way now."

"Did you tell him I was coming out to Sunland Al?"

"Yeah I did. I told him not to hurt you again. I tried to talk some sense into him. I wanted him to know that you were a fair man, that you wouldn't just shoot him. I told him about some of the cases we ran together. I thought I was going to be able to settle him down. I didn't want you to get hurt again Van. I was just stupid man. I've screwed up this whole deal. I've screwed my family and my life, it's over, done.

"Al, I promise you'll get a fair shake on this. I'll make sure your wife and kids will be taken care of. Tell me where Dutch is and we'll bring him in and put him in jail for good."

"That's just it Van. You'll try to bring Dutch in. You just don't get it do you? You're the good guy, the guy that never uses his gun. I've seen you work and I've seen Dutch work. He's slipped through the system all these years and he can do it again. You'll go by the book and Dutch will beat you. He'll kill you and Kathy. I'm responsible for this mess, and I'm going to kill him, no question. It's the only way to stop him."

"Al you'll ruin your life and your family's. Tell me where you're going."

"No more talk Van. I'll call you when I get there and you can come pick up Kathy and what's left of Dutch. I have to end this. I am so…so very sorry."

Al closes the connection and Van pounds his fist on the table.

"Damn it, son of a bitch, damn it, that stupid idiot, I swear to God I just can't stand here. I've got to do something. I can't lose Kathy. Captain can you get me one of the helicopters? I'll head east and when Al calls I'll be that much closer to him."

"Okay, I'll get you a helicopter, but don't do anything dumb. Wait for back up when you get where Dutch is. If Al is there, you have to bring him in. Don't let him out of your sight. You guys have been buddies for a long time, but you can't let him go. If Dutch is alive, I want him arrested, not killed. Use your head Van, think of Kathy. Her safety comes first. We can go downstairs and check out the box, you may still be able to use it to get Kathy."

"No I don't want the box, to hell with the box. The diamonds are glass. All this for glass, worthless glass."

"All right just be careful then. Godspeed my boy."

"Dutch doesn't walk away from me this time."

"Look, Van, all I can get on short notice is a small 'copter. If you're thinking about killing Dutch, I'm going to have a couple of officers go with you. That means a long drive by car. What's it going to be?"

"Okay, okay, I gotta have the 'copter. I meant he's not getting away again to come back and kill more people or ruin more lives. I'll do the job boss, I've got to go."

THE ARTIMUS BOX

Chapter 33

Al turns into the canyon road and calls the station to give Van the address of the house in Twentynine Palms where he is to meet Dutch with the Artimus box. Al called Dutch after he left the station. He told Dutch that he had the box and would trade it for Kathy. Dutch is sure that he has Al under his control and gives him directions to the place in Twentynine Palms.

The Captain radios Van in the helicopter to give them the location Al has given them. The helicopter is a small, but fast two-seater. Van has rushed to the waiting helicopter without his Kevlar vest, just a spare clip for his 9mm Smith and Wesson pistol.

Al turns into the small dirt road leading to the Dutch's hide out. He stops his car and takes his pistol from his holster. His plan is to shoot Dutch as soon as he sees him. He wants to get it done quickly. A loud rapping on his door window startles him. Dutch is standing by the car door grinning, with a sawed off shotgun pointed at Al's face.

"Get out of the car with your hands in plain sight. You didn't think I was gonna let you get the drop on me, did you old buddy?"

Al opens the car door with one hand and keeps the other hand raised.

"Give me your gun. I don't wanta have to shoot you before I get that box."

"I left the gun on the seat of the car, you can see it there. Where is Kathy? I want to see her safe before I give you the box."

Dutch slams the butt of the shotgun into Al's stomach, and as Al doubles over Dutch clubs him in the head. Al goes face down in the dirt. Dutch prods him with a couple of kicks to the ribs. He grabs Al's arms and flops him over onto his back.

"Don't go belly up on me old buddy, I need the box. Then I'm gonna give you another lesson on how to stay in line. Maybe you can watch me with your friend's old lady. Yeah, that's right, we'll have us a big party. You and your hero boyfriend can watch, and then you can watch me kill both of them. And then you and I can finish the party with you begging for your life. How's that sound to you big man? Hey maybe I'll let you dig graves for you and your buddies. I'd get a kick out of that, see'n you dig, see'n you sweat. You know'n I'm the man's gonna make you die."

Dutch searches Al's car. He goes through the trunk and pulls out the rear seat. He slams the cars door and smashes his fist down on the hood of the car. Dutch grabs Al by his shirt collar and drags him into the restoration shop.

He finds a length of rope and ties Al's hands together behind his back. He goes to a utility sink to run some water into a bucket. With the bucket full, he returns to Al and pours the water over Al's head. Dutch kicks him in the ribs as he is coming to.

THE ARTIMUS BOX

"That's just a taste of what you're gonna get if I don't have that box. Where's it at Al?"

"I told you I want to see Kathy first."

"I ain't playing no games here. You got the box or not?"

"I hid the box in the sand not more than a mile from here. You'll never find it if Kathy isn't safe. You let her go, and I'll take you to the box Dutch."

"I ain't lettin' you see nobody. I'm gonna beat it out of you smart boy. You always thought you were better than me. You're the good guy. I'll show you who wins in the end smart guy. I'm smarter and tougher than all you guys. Yeah, that's right, all you smart guys put together."

Dutch rages, the veins on his neck and biceps stand out with each pulse of his evil heart.

Dutch punches Al in the face. Al staggers back against a wooden column trying to keep his balance. Dutch rushes forward and delivers another blow before Al can react. Al, already woozy from the shotgun blow to the head, slides down the column to the floor. As Al goes down, his binding snags an electrical switch box lever. The shops' huge electric motor comes to life. The ceiling shafts begin to turn and the big leather belts bounce and slap the driven pulleys of the machines. Dutch stands over Al laughing.

"Oh yeah, you're real tough amigo. For as big as you are, you go down easy. Now I want that box, or I'm gonna start cuttin' on your face."

Dutch kicks Al in the stomach and Al curls up in a tight ball. Dutch pulls out his big knife as he reaches down to pull Al up. While protecting himself from receiving blows in a fetal position, he struggles to get a small .32 caliber pistol out of his ankle holster.

Al twists around and fires the pistol at Dutch. He hits Dutch in the side with one wild shot and is trying to line up another shot when Dutch throws his knife into Al's chest. Dutch roars in anger and triumph; he rips the knife from Al's chest. Al's eyes flicker; he fires the pistol twice more.

Dutch lurches back as one bullet hits him in the leg. One of the flapping leather belts snags his torn shirt. The belt yanks at his huge arm; he jerks free and windmills his arms as he tries to keep his balance. Falling backwards, he smashes his head into a corner of a huge old cast iron lathe bed. Knocked out by the blow, Dutch falls to the floor of the shop. Blood spreads from his head wound to form a small pool that leaches into the old wood floor.

Chapter 34

Outside the sound of a helicopter fades as it lands nearby. Van jumps from the helicopter before its skids touch the ground, the rotors still spinning. He ducks his head, pulls his pistol and runs for the shop where he can hear the commotion of the machinery. Van moves cautiously into the building and sees Al lying motionless by a support column and Dutch lying on the floor across from Al, blood pooling by his head.

Van scans the rest of the shop, then turns around, and runs to the small house. Van slams through the front door, looks around and goes through a curtained archway to find Kathy struggling with the tape that is binding her to the bed. Van very gently removes the tape that covers his wife's bruised mouth. Kathy starts to cry and Van's eyes well up. He uses his small penknife to cut away the rest of the tape holding Kathy to the bed. Van hugs Kathy and kisses her. Kathy hugs Van around his neck as if she will never let go.

"Are you okay baby? God I'm happy to see you. I have never been so lost in all my life. Did he hurt you?"

"I'm not hurt. Just please let me go to the bathroom and then I need to drink some water."

Van helps Kathy up, and with his arm around her waist for support, he walks her to the bathroom.

"If you'll be all right for a minute, I'll go out to the shop and see about Al. Will you be ok for a couple of minutes?"

"Is Al with you? I heard gunshots. Is Al okay?"

"He's lying on the floor of the shop and Dutch is lying across from him. I think they killed each other."

"Oh my god, not Al. Please go see if you can help him, I'll be fine here."

"I'm going but not till you promise to stay here. The man with the helicopter is waiting for you. When you can get on your feet, go past the shop entrance and over the little hill between the Joshua trees. Don't come in the shop. Please do as I say. Okay?"

After getting Kathy some water, Van goes back to the shop. He walks through the door and sees Al still lying where he was. The machinery is still sending the belts snapping, and slapping, around the pulley system. Dutch is gone.

Van turns around quickly, to get back to Kathy and finds Dutch standing in the doorway, a huge knife in his hand. Van pulls his pistol and points it at Dutch. Dutch has blood running down his left arm and more blood down his right side. His face has blood running down it from his scalp. He is a huge ugly mass of wild hatred.

Van shouts over the din of the machinery. "Put the knife down Dutch. It's all over. I'm going to take you in."

"What are you gonna do, boy scout, shoot me? Al told me you were his hero, man, but that was before I killed him. See I can kill all you pigs; you can't stand up to me. He said you never used your gun to catch bad

THE ARTIMUS BOX

guys. He said you used your head instead, but you ain't no smarter than me pig. I think you just ain't got the cojones man. You ever shot that thing at anything but paper targets man? I'm gonna finish you and get back to the little woman." Dutch steps closer to Van.

"Stay where you are. You're never going to see my wife again, you low life moron. That was the last mistake you're ever going to make. What you're going to do is die in prison, and I'll be there to watch, or you're going to die right here and I'm going to do it. So lie down on the ground and put your hands behind your back."

"Oh yeah I'm the moron. You're the big man here, the big hero. Just let me get my hands on you little man. You can't make me lie down asshole, you think you can put my face in the dirt. All you guys ain't noth'n after I get done. Just like your buddy Al here, you can't stand up to me, you punks ain't noth'n." Dutch spits blood from his mouth, as he shuffles his feet to close the distance.

"You're not getting your hands on me Dutch. Don't you get it? That's all you've got, just some drug-induced muscle, most of it between your ears. You're pathetic. Tell me Einstein, was this murderous rampage of yours all because of the Artimus box?"

"The box, that damned box. If I coulda got it, I coulda had the whole West Coast trade man. I got papers over in that pile of stuff that says that box is full of diamonds. Your dead friend buried it somewhere out in the desert man. Ain't no one ever goin' to find it. Them diamonds are gone man. Come on pig, you gonna talk me to death or what? You ain't gonna do it man; you ain't gonna shoot me."

He takes another tentative step as if while he is talking, Van will not notice he is coming closer. The thought of killing Van is all Dutch's demented brain can think about. He tastes the blood in his mouth. He thinks he'll kill this cop and then go after the rich punks on the list he got from Manley. He'll get his money and make the big deals, kill and make the big deals. No one can stop him.

"I've got the box Linus. The diamonds are fake glass, as worthless as you are. You know, just like you Limpter, a stupid box of rocks."

"You lousy bastard." Dutch lunges forward raising his arm to throw the knife. The two men are now less than eight feet apart. Van has a perfect target picture. He does not hesitate, he fires three quick shots. The first two drill through Dutch's heart, the third shot tears through his neck. Dutch looks at Van with an expression of disbelief. Van steps back as Dutch crashes flat on his face to the floor…dead.

"This is one time the gun was the best remedy Limpter, like putting down a rabid dog."

Van walks over to Al, kneels down to feel for his pulse. The beat of life is gone from his friend. Van leaves the shop and walks back to the house. Kathy runs to Van and throws her arms around him.

"Is it over Van? I thought that maniac would kill all of us. Oh is…is Al gone?"

"Dutch has been sent to hell where he belongs, but he took too many people with him. Yes Al's dead."

THE ARTIMUS BOX

Epilogue

Van and the Captain have kept quiet about Al's involvement during the official inquiry. The police force turns out to bury Al Lieber with full honors. The police commission awards his wife and children the full pension.

An officer involved shooting inquiry clears Van in the shooting. He is thinking again about retiring. Van is not happy about killing Dutch, but he has promised Kathy and himself that he will not beat himself up over it.

The probate court awarded The Kim Derby Artimus collection to his former wife. She quickly decided to put the entire collection up for auction. Malcolm Donner fought off numerous bidders in a high stakes bidding war to win the bulk of the collection. Van and Kathy were present at the auction and Donner asked if they would come to his home for a celebration after he had sorted through the collection.

The next weekend Van and Kathy go to Malcolm Donner's house to celebrate with him. Malcolm greets them at the door and, with great fanfare, invites them in. Malcolm seems very excited and happy. They go into the study where Donner's housekeeper, Mrs.

Lansing, is placing hors d'oeuves on a table and bottles of champagne in buckets of ice.

"Wow Malcolm this is quite a spread. You must really be happy with the collection."

"I am very happy Van, but not only with the new collection. I wanted to have you and Kathy here to tell you that I finally have gotten the nerve to ask Mrs. Lansing, Esther is her lovely name, to be my wife. She has accepted and we are to be married in the spring. We both want you two to be our honored guests at the wedding."

"Malcolm, Esther, congratulations. We are delighted. You make a wonderful couple."

Kathy hugs Esther. Malcolm and Van shake hands. Malcolm opens the first bottle of champagne and pours the golden bubbly into glasses.

"I have sorted out the collection I bought at the auction and have found some items from Harry Artimus that no one knew existed. The most important to me is the Artimus Journal. It is the first known example of any journal writing done by Harry Artimus. It is also important to us as it explains a great deal of the over seventy years' old Artimus box mystery."

"We know that Tim Wahl was killed for the box in 1932. We now know that Dutch killed Kim Derby in 1998 for this journal and the rest of the collection, and I believe Phil Manley was also responsible. Dutch and Manley believed that the box contained diamonds worth millions."

"After I read the journal, and from what you told me Van, I believe that all but three of the diamonds were fakes.

THE ARTIMUS BOX

I think Harry Artimus found out the diamonds were mostly fakes and that he took the three real ones. One of the diamonds Harry had set into a necklace; he gave it to his wife Mae as a present. I think he sold the other two. Harry, in the end of this journal, states that when Kline finds the fake diamonds he will know the joke. This was probably Harry's way of slapping Kline in the face for all the lies and deceit. I am positive that Harry must have suspected that Kline had something to do with Tim Wahl's disappearance. He must have wondered if Kline ever found the box and the fake diamonds."

"I have donated the journal and some of Harry's personal items that I have to the museum in Washington D.C. I wanted everyone interested in early American racing to be able to see the richness of Harry's works. I have not been able to force myself to give away all of my collection.

"I want to enjoy it while I can. I enjoy having people come here to study the collection and to talk about what it means to them. Upon my passing, all of the collection will go to the museum and be displayed for the public."

"Well, Malcolm, I think you have answered all of the questions that I had concerning the Artimus case. I'm glad that it's over. It always amazes me what greed will do to people, all the killing and lies. I don't want to put a damper on your good fortune, so I'll stop with the crime comments.

"Kathy and I really enjoy your company. We appreciate that as one of the good things that came from this case. We are going to take a long vacation and relax. After that, I think we'll see if retirement is what we want to do. We will make sure to be back for your wedding."

Malcolm says, "Here is to all of us; to the end of a tragedy and the beginning of a new life."

###

Thank you for reading THE ARTIMUS BOX. I hope you enjoyed it.

My next novel, NOVAC'S RACE, takes place in the 1930's with Jack Novac, an Indy 500 winner, going to Europe. Trouble follows Jack wherever he goes. Jack fights back by breaking speed records at every race track until he runs up against an Italian team bent on teaching him a lesson.

You can read the first chapter on my website, http://www.mikedownsmysteries.com.

Connect with me on online
Facebook: Mike Downs
Twitter:@Mike Downs Author
Goodreads: Mike Downs

About the Author

I started racing for Group 44, the factory Triumph sports car team on the East Coast. After winning a national championship I moved to California to race the new Titan Formula Ford for the West Coast distributor.

I raced for forty years in Trans Am, IMSA, Formula Atlantic, and FIA endurance races. I drove factory cars for Triumph, Porsche, Datsun, and Titan. I won the last championship with a sports car I designed and built at my company, Downs Engineering. Downs Engineering builds race cars, specialty cars, and Hayabusa racing engines. Please visit http://www.downsengineering.com website.

I live in Northern California with my lovely wife, Kathy.

Made in the USA
Charleston, SC
24 January 2012